Emmerdale Farm Book 12
Face Value

They strolled hand in hand down to the village then on up the lane, hardly taking note of their steps. Matt was trying to think of a way to ask Dolly if she was happy at Emmerdale. To him it seemed an odd thing to be asking.

She loved him, he was sure of that. She had told him so. When he asked her to marry him, he'd explained his role as partner in Emmerdale Farm. She surely understood that his home was Emmerdale. How could she be 'restless'?

'You know, Dolly,' he began, 'that six thousand pounds that came to me just afore we got married?'

'Yes,' she said absently, tweaking a leaf from the hedge as they walked, 'what about it?'

'How would you feel about taking it out and putting it as a deposit on a house?'

There was a pause. Then, with a reaction that astounded him, she flung her arms round him and hugged him hard. When she let him go, he saw tears glinting in her eyes.

'Oh, Matt!' she whispered. 'I'd just love to have a little house of our own.'

LEE MACKENZIE

Face Value

Emmerdale Farm Book 12

Based on the successful
❤ Yorkshire Television series
originated by Kevin Laffan

FONTANA/Collins

First published by Fontana Paperbacks 1980
Third impression April 1986

Made and printed in Great Britain by
William Collins Sons & Co Ltd, Glasgow

Chapter One

The people of Beckindale were expecting changes on the Verney Estate, of course. When Mr Verney's marriage broke up and he moved away to live in France, there had been a lot of talk about buying the Hall to use as a community centre. The county council hadn't had the money in the end, so the next thing was that the house would be used as a teacher training college. In fact, it was used for one or two weekend seminars but never became a regular college.

'A waste, is that,' Sam Pearson remarked when the subject came up in the Woolpack. 'Fine old house, full of fine things. Should be used.'

But for the most part, Beckindale folk were happy enough to leave everything as it was. Many of the farms in the dale were rented from the Verney Estate. Best not to change things . . . who could tell what a new landlord would be like?

Then . . . sensation . . . The *Hotten Courier* carried a notice that Mr George Verney of Verney Hall in Beckindale had died in Cannes. 'Hey-up, Amos, why didn't thee tell us he'd gone?' grumbled the customers in the pub. 'Should've sent a wreath or summat, shouldn't us?'

'Ah, well, see,' murmured Amos Brearley, looking knowing, 'a French funeral, y'see. Different, is that.'

'No wreaths?'

'Of course they have wreaths,' snorted old Sam. 'Saw 'em when I was in France in t'First War. Horses wi' black plumes, and gurt black ribbons on t'hearse, and everybody in black – take it a lot more serious than we do, if you want my opinion.' He sipped his drink then gave Amos a sharp glance from his light blue eyes. 'Truth is, you didn't know. That's it, isn't it, Amos?'

He was right. But Amos didn't want that bruited abroad. As representative of the *Hotten Courier* in Beckindale, he felt it part of his role to know everything that was going to appear in the newspaper. It added to his prestige to be thought of as a part of the great journalistic network that reached to London and beyond.

5

'The information didn't reach my newspaper until after the funeral rites,' he said in a lofty tone, pulling down the fronts of his cardigan and looking dignified. 'First the French authorities, then the British Ambassador –'

'Consul, you mean,' put in Sam.

'Er . . . aye . . . consul,' agreed Amos. 'Slip of the tongue.' Ambassador, consul . . . he'd never had dealings with either. 'Any road, by the time the Verney solicitors were informed and so on, it were a bit late for letting folks know they should send a wreath. But you can rely on t'*Courier* to keep us up to date as far as can be managed when dealing with foreigners.'

'What I want to know,' said Henry Wilks, joining Amos in the bar after clearing some cluttered tables, 'is what happens next? Who inherits? Anyone know?'

'Well, he'd no son,' Sam pointed out. 'That flighty wife o' his . . . Wouldn't have childer, he as good as told me that once. At sheepdog trials, it were. George Verney had a dog entered. He used to take an interest in the home farm then – that bit of a farm that Clissold uses now for grazing. Verney had sheep on it, an' a dog . . . What were its name, now?' He called across the room to his grandson Joe, who was deep in a pint and a discussion about Manchester United. 'Hi, Joe, what were the name of Verney's dog?'

'Eh?'

'That dog. Entered for trials just before we lost Patch.'

'Oh, that one.' Joe got up and sauntered to the counter. 'You mean the one he had the summer our Jack came home and fell for Mrs Verney.'

Old Sam went red. 'Nay, then, Joe! No need to drag that up!'

Joe grinned, teeth very white in a tanned face. 'One o' the most interesting things that ever happened in Beckindale,' he said. 'It even shook up Mr Verney!'

The group at the bar looked at each other in mixed embarrassment and amusement. They all remembered that summer perfectly. Joe's elder brother Jack Sugden had come home to get away from the unexpected pressures of being a bestselling novelist and, with his usual luck where women were concerned, had attracted the eye of Mrs Verney. Much younger than her husband and a 'townie', Mrs Verney had been bored almost out of her mind by Beckindale and all that

6

went with it until Jack happened along. George Verney had reacted in a most satisfactory fashion, as far as onlookers were concerned: he'd actually given Jack Sugden a public horsewhipping.

Well, that had been four years ago, or thereabouts. It seemed to be the deathknell of the marriage. The erring wife had packed up and gone to London, Mr Verney hung around getting more grey and silent, and then he too had moved away. He'd lost interest in the dale. Time was when he'd been a part of the local life, but not for a long time now.

'Happen it's as well somebody new will take on,' Henry said. 'There's a couple of tenant farmers on Verney Estate that could do with a bit of a shake-up – *somebody* ought to do summat about the drainage on t'west slope, and as to those tied cottages attached to Maidstowe Farm . . . they're a disgrace.'

'You're right,' Joe said. 'I know for a fact that Bill Dixon at Maidstowe has been writing to the Verney solicitors for over a year, trying to get agreement to apply for an improvement grant and all that rubbish. From what I can gather, Mr Verney just didn't answer letters sent on to him from Hotten. Unfair, is that. You can't expect a farmer to manage his affairs if his landlord won't answer letters.'

'Thank heaven we own Emmerdale,' Henry said. 'Couldn't be doing with that – asking somebody else for permission to do summat, and having to cool your heels while you wait for an answer.'

Joe nodded agreement. Five years had gone by since Henry Wilks had bought the freehold of Emmerdale Farm, thus buying himself into a partnership with the owners of the Verney lease. Joe's father Jacob had just died, leaving his affairs in something of a mess. What was worse, he'd left the farm – that's to say, the lease and the livestock and the equipment – to his eldest child Jack who was nowhere to be found.

At that time Henry Wilks had just come to live in Beckindale with his daughter Marion. Henry had retired early from the business of making money in chemicals and allied products, fancying himself as a rural landlord. But retirement hung heavy on his hands so that when he discovered Jack Sugden didn't want his inheritance and

7

problems were gathering thick and fast for the Emmerdale family, it seemed a good idea to buy himself into the farming life.

They were now equal partners: Henry, Annie Sugden, her son Joe and her son-in-law Matt who had inherited a share on the death of his wife Peggy. The agreement whereby they'd gone into partnership and the contract for the purchase of the farm from George Verney had been complicated – many a local sage had prophesied trouble at the idea of four people managing a farm. But it had worked. Emmerdale was one of the best farms in the dale.

Others in the Woolpack joined in the discussion about the Verney Estate. Everyone had an opinion or so-called inside information. But in fact for the next few weeks nothing else happened. And when the next step came, it was once again from the *Hotten Courier* that they learned the facts.

'Death Duties Burden Verney Legacy', announced the headline with, in smaller type below it, 'Verney Heir's Problem.' The piece went on to say that the heir was George Verney's nephew Gerald, director of a small import-export business in London. There were two or three paragraphs about the financial outlook: 'The revenue men are asking for a sum that's quite out of the question,' Gerald Verney was reported as saying, then went on to remark that he made a comfortable living from dealing in industrial solvents but couldn't afford to meet the tax from his own funds.

That point wasn't pursued for the moment. What interested the Beckindalers was that he was said to be about to visit the estate and bring his wife with him. His wife, it was noted, was an earl's daughter.

'There now,' Sam grunted when he read it. 'That's more like it, Annie. We'll have folks living in the Hall again.'

Annie put his mid-morning coffee at his elbow. 'I've only put in one spoon of sugar,' she said. 'You're still sticking to your notion of cutting down, are you?'

'Annie!' Sam exclaimed. 'Aren't you interested in what I'm telling thee? Mr Verney and his wife are coming to the Hall.'

'Aye,' she said. Her calm, handsome face was thoughtful.

'Well? Won't that be fine? I hope this Gerald will take up the home farm again. Clissold doesn't really need that

8

grazing. Great, isn't it? The Verneys have always been interested in sheep and sheepdogs. D'you recall they had two champions? There was that little 'un – Maze, wasn't that her name? And then that dog they brought in from Wales. I don't remember what that one was called. Bach? Bryn? Summat o't'sort.'

'Aye,' Annie said again.

Sam eyed her. 'What's wrong? I thought you'd be pleased. Having a lady up at t'Hall would make life a lot simpler for you, now wouldn't it? She'd take on a lot of t'things you've been landed with recently just because you're church-warden. I mean, welfare things that aren't really proper to churchwardening . . .'

'Dad,' Annie began, rather dubiously. 'I've read the paper. It only says the Verneys are to visit. It says nowt about them settling in.'

'Oh, but they will. That's what they're coming for, isn't it? To take a look and see what they need to do.'

'That's the point, Dad. There's a lot needs doing. The place has been more or less empty for four years. You know yourself there are slates gone off the roof, and the damp got in –'

'Oh, that's easily seen to –'

'But don't you remember . . . Mrs George Verney kept on saying it needed a fortune spent on it just to keep it heated . . . And heating's gone up an awful lot since then –'

'Oh, rubbish! All those open fires and things – ! This new lad will put in a few radiators and sort it in no time.'

Annie shook her head. She wasn't so sure. 'Don't you notice the paper says he's got a small business in London? He wouldn't want to come north to live, happen.'

'Of course he'll want to,' Sam insisted stoutly. To him it was self-evident. Any man who inherited a house like the Hall was bound to want to live in it. After all, that was what the Hall was all about, wasn't it? Inheritance, tradition, continuance . . . No Verney worth his salt would turn his back on the place. True, Mr George had left the dale, but that was because of that unsuitable wife of his. The new one was different – an earl's daughter . . . That was the right stuff. Oh, everything would be different in Beckindale once the Hall had occupants. There would be somebody to give the prizes at the Horticultural Show and to take over the chairmanship of the Hunt and to set standards of morals and manners.

Matt and Joe were told all about it when they came in for their elevenses. 'How old is he, this new Verney?' Joe enquired.

'What's it matter how old he is?'

'I wondered what Mrs Verney was going to be like. Last one was a right handicap, wasn't she? If the new one prefers London to Beckindale, it's a dead loss, Grandad.'

'Mr Gerald Verney, aged thirty-five, of Precosolv Ltd,' Matt read out. 'Precosolv, what's that, for goodness' sake?'

No one knew. Henry was able to give the information when he turned up for lunch soon after midday. 'Saw it in the *Courier*,' he said, 'so I made a few enquiries. It's a decentish firm that brings in gums and oils from the Mediterranean for making liquid soaps.'

Joe chuckled, and Sam looked annoyed. A soap importer hardly seemed quite the right sort of person for occupancy of the Hall. 'Makes shampoo, does he?' Joe said.

'Nay, he's not in manufacture. He just buys and sells ingredients, arranges for their carriage to folks that need 'em. Not a bad little business. Not much competition, I s'pose, and probably not much in the way of pressure or crisis. No, I'd say Mr Gerald Verney is on to a nice little number there.'

'So it's the kind of thing he could leave to his . . . er . . . subordinates if he came to live in Beckindale?' Sam enquired.

'Oh, aye. Run down to London once a week, mebbe – just to keep an eye on things. Aye, not a bad set-up. Have you heard he's going to move in, then?'

'Dad's taking it for granted that's what the report means,' Annie put in with a slight frown of warning at her son. She didn't want Joe to rag her father about this. He might not think it was important, but Sam did. Sam remembered the days when he himself had worked for the Verneys, who were then folk of weight and authority.

'Of course I'm taking it for granted,' Sam declared. 'He's a Verney, isn't he? It's his duty to take on the responsibilities. When he comes, I must just have a word wi' him – tell him I used to work for his great-uncle, that I remember how things used to be and he can rely on me for hints and memories about how the place was run.'

'He'd get that from the solicitors, surely, Sam?' Henry said. Henry had a crease between his grey eyebrows. He wasn't as confident as Sam that the Hall could be restored to its former glory.

'Nay, what do them fellers know?' Sam snorted. 'They know the money side, of course, I'm not denying that. But I know how the party was run on New Year's Day when the tenants came in to pay their rent. I know how much hay they used to get off the north fields, as compared to the southfacing ones. I know where they got the anthracite from that made the boiler work at its best temperature. T'only other person in Beckindale who knows as much as I do about the old Verney household is Alice Tooker, and she's so deaf you can't hold a conversation wi' her.'

Henry still looked dubious. Later, when Sam had gone out to his vegetable garden and the young men were off tinkering with the tractor, Annie and Dolly set about the washing-up with Henry putting the dishes away.

'You didn't say much at dinner when Grandad were on about the Hall,' Dolly remarked to him.

'Thought it best not.'

'What is it, Henry?' Annie asked, pausing with a saucepan halfway into the water. 'You've got summat on your mind.'

'It's the death duties, Annie. I saw more details of the estate finances in the *Guardian* a few weeks ago, and the way it struck me, that Verney lad is going to have his work cut out to find the money.'

'But Mr Verney – the one that died – he left some money, didn't he? He must have had money,' Dolly said in a tone of reason. 'He couldn't have afforded to live on the Riviera if he hadn't.'

'You're right, Dolly. But an income sufficient to give you a pleasant enough life isn't the same thing as a lump sum to pay to the tax man. Capital transfer can amount to a huge sum.'

'Capital transfer?'

'We usually call it "death duties". It's really the capital transfer tax. It'd be payable when property changes hands but in the case of the death of a landowner, we still call it "death duties". What I'm saying, Annie, is that I wonder if Gerald Verney could *afford* to live at the Hall – if he'd have enough left after the tax.'

'Dad's going to be disappointed if he doesn't,' Annie said with wry amusement. 'He's taking it quite personally!'

'It's nice, is that,' Dolly said. 'In a town, hardly anybody cares who moves in up the top of the road!'

'That's why you married Matt, is it?' teased Henry. 'So you could get involved with the lord of the manor?'

'I had another reason, but don't let on to Matt,' she replied, twinkling.

'Nay, lass, he doesn't need anyone to tell him. It's there in your face every time you look at him.'

Dolly gained a little colour and turned away. 'It's not fair,' she said, halfway between pleasure and embarrassment. 'I can't help having a face that shows how I feel!'

'Dunno why you sound so regretful about it. I reckon you and Matt are two of the luckiest folk I know.'

'Well, if it's true, Henry, it's *time* Matt had a bit of luck,' Dolly replied.

'Nobody will argue with you on that. So now, Annie, where does this gurt dish go?'

'Top shelf above the dresser, Henry,' Annie told him. She smiled fondly at Dolly. 'Off you go, lass. That's chores done for the time being.'

Dolly nodded and went out into the sweet sunshine of early summer. The birds were still singing, keen to gain and hold their territory for the nesting season that had just begun. The trees were fresh in their greenery, unspoilt yet by dust and heat. She could here the tractor chugging stolidly on the far field over towards Grey Top – it seemed the fault had been cured and the men had taken it off to test it.

She intended to ask Mr Pearson for permission to gather some flowers for the house, but Sam had wandered off on some ploy of his own after examining the rows for signs of carrot fly or aphid. Dolly moved among the neat plots of the vegetable garden to the section where Sam had set ground aside for flowers. He was a great flower-grower, was Sam – he won prizes at the Show with his dahlias and roses.

The air was full of a rich, sweet scent. She threaded her way between the rows until she found the source – it was the trellis of canes and string where the sweet peas were growing. How beautiful they were! Like butterflies turned into flowers – deep purple, pale blue, carmine, rose-pink, vermilion. She leaned close to breathe in the scent, then made up her mind. These were the flowers she'd take indoors – there were plenty of them, and they would fill the house with perfume as well as look lovely in the crystal vase.

She had the kitchen scissors in the pocket of her apron. She cut flowers with care, choosing long stems and from among the clumps where they grew thickest. Before long she had as many as she could carry in one hand. She was holding them out to admire them when she heard a step behind her and turned to find Joe.

'Hello,' she said. 'Tractor okay?'

'Aye, not bad. Come back to make a few phone calls.'

'Matt still up there?'

'He's started cutting grass.'

'For silage?'

Joe grinned. 'We'll turn you into a farmer's wife yet!' he said with approval.

'I *am* a farmer's wife.'

'You can't say that until you've been dragged out of bed to help look after a calving cow, or taken two or three lambs into your kitchen for bottle-feeding.'

'Oh, thanks!'

'No, but seriously, Dolly – you liking it all right?'

'Liking it?' she breathed. 'Oh . . . that's not the word for it.'

Joe nodded, then his brown eyes lit up with mischief. 'You'll get that rapturous look wiped off your face if Grandad catches you.'

'Eh?' gasped Dolly, startled. For Sam in his wrath was alarming. 'Now what have I done?'

'Asked permission to pick them sweet peas, did you?'

'Er . . . no . . . well, I'd mentioned to your Ma that I was going to pick some flowers.'

Joe pulled a doleful face and hunched his shoulders. 'Rather you than me, then,' he said, and walked away.

Dolly stood with the bunch of sweet peas in her hand. 'Oh *dear*,' she sighed.

In fact, no harm came of it. Sam was kind to her. 'It's just I like to pick sweet peas atween six and seven in the evening,' he said. 'Cool of the day, see? They've had a day's nourishment in the sun and the soil, then you pick 'em and take 'em indoors for a good drink when it's cool.'

'I'm sorry, Mr Pearson. I didn't know . . .'

'That's all right, lass. Flowers are for giving folks pleasure, after all. I like to see them appreciated. But they ought to be given the best chance to do well when you pick 'em, see?'

'Yes. I won't do it again.'

But Sam wasn't put out. He was in a good mood at the moment. The Verneys were coming back to the Hall, God was in his heaven, all was right with the world.

This euphoria continued for several days, though it was somewhat dashed when Gerald Verney actually turned up in Beckindale. Sam had made it his business to keep an eye on the Hall in his daily walks, so he saw the car drive into the grounds – a car he didn't recognize. What's more, someone had clearly been there beforehand to unlock the old gates by the gatehouse. Sam was on the slope of the valley above the river, but his sight was good. He saw the man get out of the car and pause to stare at the front of the house. Then someone else came out of the front door to shake hands with him. Sam studied the two men. One was tubby, balding, in a shabby tweed suit. The other was tall and rather impressive, with dark hair coming down to a point on his forehead – the Verney hairline, without a doubt.

That must be Gerald Verney!

Beside himself with excitement, Sam went hurrying down the slope into the village. His first thought was to rush to the Hall and introduce himself to the new owner, but as he walked he decided that was not fitting. He, after all, had only been a stockman on the Verney Estate and was now only an elder of the village. Someone with more dignity and authority ought to welcome Mr Verney to Beckindale on behalf of its inhabitants.

The obvious choice was the vicar. Sam marched quickly by the Woolpack, across the green, up Vicarage Lane. Henry Wilks, setting ash trays on tables in preparation for the morning opening of the pub, caught a glimpse of him as he hustled past the windows of the Woolpack. Something

14

important must be happening to make Sam step it out like that.

It so happened that Annie Sugden was with the vicar, having a discussion about transport for the Sunday School outing. Sam hustled in through the ever open door of the vicarage to interrupt this weighty discussion. 'Vicar! Oh – Annie – you're here too! Well, that's all to the good. Vicar, what d'you think? Gerald Verney's up at t'Hall.'

'Is he?' Hinton got up, surprised. 'How do you know, Sam?'

'I saw 'un! Got out of his car. Unmistakable.'

'Well, you always said he'd come, didn't you. Sit down, Sam. You look hot and flustered. Would you like some tea?'

'Nay, there's no time for that. Listen, vicar, you'd best get up there to see him.'

Donald Hinton raised thick black eyebrows at this remark. 'Me? But . . . why should I do that, Sam?'

'Well, we've got to give him a welcome, haven't we? It's only right. The Verneys have come home again. We've got to show we value them. So just put your jacket on, vicar, and get up to the Hall and tell him that on behalf of the village you – '

'One moment, Sam,' said Mr Hinton, holding up a hand. He glanced at Annie, who was speechless with surprise at her father's suggestion. Hinton's look asked her for her opinion. She gathered her wits and gave a tiny shake of the head. Hinton went on, thus encouraged: 'I don't think we ought to rush into an act like that, Sam. In the first place, we've had no prior information of the visit so it seems clear Verney didn't expect anything of the kind. And then, you see – we don't even know it really is Gerald Verney.'

'Oh, it's him,' Sam insisted. 'He's got the widow's peak.' He sketched it with his thumb on his own forehead. 'Besides, he's tall and squarish – the family resemblance is unmistakable.'

'But Dad,' Annie began, finding her voice, 'I don't know that it's up to us to hurry there and make speeches of welcome. Oughtn't we to wait until we're invited there?'

'Rubbish! Old Mr Verney were never one to stand on ceremony.'

'But this isn't old Mr Verney. This isn't even our "young

Mr Verney". This is some young man we've never met at all, from London. How do we know he wants or expects a committee of welcome?'

Sam hesitated. 'We-ell . . . happen he wouldn't know what to expect. But we ought to show him we're glad he's come back. We want them back at the Hall, don't we? It's up to us to show him we'll do all we can to make him feel at home.'

The vicar paused a moment in thought. 'I agree we ought to show him we would welcome him,' he murmured. 'But it hardly seems quite right to hurry there the moment he puts his nose round the door.'

'That's not how I see it,' Sam said. 'The sooner we shake him by the hand, the better he'll know our feelings.'

'Well, if he comes into the village, of course we'll approach him – '

'That's not the way it ought to be!' Sam objected. 'We ought to go there – say a few words – official, like.'

'But Sam, nobody has delegated us to do any such thing.'

'Goodness gracious, vicar, we don't need an Act of Parliament for a thing like this. Of course the folks of the village would want us to go . . .'

'You may be right in saying they'd want some words of welcome offered, Sam. But whether they'd choose *me* to utter them . . .'

'Of course they'd choose you. You're t'vicar, aren't you?'

'But there's the chairman of the parish council, Sam.'

'Oh, *him*.' Sam paused. 'Any road, he's at work in his garage in Hotten. We're *here*. We should get up there and say – '

'I think it could come better from the chairman or a member of the parish council.'

'Nonsense. Vicar and churchwarden – that's good enough, surely?'

Hinton shook his head. 'I don't think I'd care to rush into this, Sam,' he said with firmness. 'I agree it would probably be a good action to say some words of welcome to Mr Verney, but I don't think they have to be said the moment he appears, and I'm not going to take it on myself to say them without consulting others.'

'You mean you won't go?'

Hinton hesitated then shook his head. 'I would rather not.'

'Oh, good heavens,' Sam said in high irritation. 'I'm just wasting time here, then.' He turned and marched out again, banging his walking stick on the hall tiles as he departed.

The vicar looked at Annie. 'Should I go after him?'

She shook her head. 'Don't worry. He won't go up there on his own – never was one for making speeches or taking a public stance. He may go into Hotten to see Norman Harrolds.'

'That would be better. I'd far rather have the chairman of the parish council take on this chore.'

They discussed it for a few more moments then went back to the problem of the coach firm. Sam meanwhile had trudged back to the Woolpack and knocked on the door.

'We're not open yet,' Amos Brearley called through the door.

'It's me, Amos. Open up, I want to talk to Henry.'

Amos debated whether to tell Sam to go round to the back door, which was unlocked, but decided it would be easier to open up at the front. He locked up again as soon as Sam stepped inside. There was a quarter of an hour to go till opening time, and Amos was a stickler for the letter of the law.

'Henry!' Sam shouted.

'Do you mind?' Amos said. 'That was right in my ear!'

Henry appeared from the kitchen, where he was preparing a joint of lamb to go into the oven for lunch. 'Hello, Sam,' he said, half in and half out of the doorway, his eye still on his work. 'Saw you go steaming past a while ago. Something up?'

'Gerald Verney's arrived at the Hall,' Sam burst out. 'Listen, Henry, it's up to us to give him a welcome. You've got to tidy yourself up and go there to have a word with him.'

'Me?' gasped Henry, coming out into the bar.

'Yes, you.' Sam advanced on him, pointing a finger like the poster of Kitchener. 'Come on now, take off that apron and let's get up there.'

'I'm doing no such thing,' Henry said, more curtly than he intended. 'What on earth do I want to go up there for?'

'Well, you're a leading citizen of Beckindale, aren't you?'

17

'I don't know so much about that. Besides, I've got something to do here.'

'You know as well as I do, Henry – when a speech is wanted at a dance or a concert, you're the one that's asked to make it. And you gave the prizes at the Flower Show last year . . .'

'That's an entirely different thing from making a speech of welcome to a man I never met and know nothing about. Besides, how do I know the rest of Beckindale would want that?'

'Certainly they'd want it.'

'I don't know so much,' Amos put in. 'I mean, no disrespect, Mr Wilks, but there are others . . .'

'Too right there are,' Henry agreed in a forceful tone. He frowned at Sam. 'Did you just go up to the vicarage?'

'Well . . . yes.'

'To ask the vicar to do this speech of welcome?'

'Ye-es.'

'And he said no.'

'He's . . . in the middle of a discussion with Annie – '

'And I'm in the middle of tying a crown of lamb.'

'Don't talk so daft, Henry! As if that matters.'

'It matters to me, price lamb is these days.' Besides, Henry was saying to himself, this is the twentieth century. The time's gone by when you welcomed the squire with touching of the forelock. *I'm* not going up there to kow-tow to the Verneys. I'm surprised Sam thinks it's proper.

Sam, as if he had heard this internal monologue, said on a quiet, rather sad note, 'I want the man to feel wanted, Henry. When that big house up there is empty, it's like a . . . a hole in the wall of our local society. Warmth and friendship seem to seep away through it. When the Verneys were there, they gave parties and had folk there for discussion of local affairs, and the Hunt met there, and the mummers used to perform there, and they always came to the Nativity Play, and could be relied on to open a fête or judge a competition . . . So you see . . .'

Henry relented. He put a hand on Sam's arm. 'I see what you mean, Sam. But honest, I don't think it's up to me to take any steps. I mean to say, I'm one of the most recent incomers to Beckindale.'

'Oh, now, don't talk daft. You're one of us now. It would come well from you, Henry. 'Sides, you've got experience of business and that kind of thing. You could chat wi' him about it.'

Although Henry could see what lay behind Sam's idea, he was determined not to go. Gerald Verney would think he was out of his mind, arriving unannounced and bowing and scraping. He shook his head. 'No, Sam, I just don't think I'm the right man, and I'm not even sure it's a good idea in itself.'

'Oh, I don't know so much,' suggested Amos, who'd been attending to all this with extreme interest. 'I think it would be a suitable move, to greet the new owner of the Verney Estate. And you know, as owner of the local inn – '

Henry stared at Amos, aghast. Then he turned to Sam as if to say, 'Now look what you've done.'

Sam said hastily, 'Happen it's not such a good idea. Vicar were against it, and Annie were against it, and now Henry is against it.'

'But that doesn't mean that two responsible persons like you and me, Mr Pearson – '

'Nay, Amos, I've gone off the whole thing,' Sam said in a testy manner, and went out.

Henry hesitated, then pulled off his apron and hurried after him. Normally it was best to let the old fellow get over his moods without interfering, but there had been something so wistful about him when he spoke of the old days that Henry sensed he would be downcast now.

Amos watched him go, not even troubling to complain at the way he abandoned preparations for their lunch.

Then he went to the phone and rang the *Hotten Courier*. The editor sighed a little at hearing his voice. 'Yes, what is it?' he asked.

'Er . . . listen . . . it seems like Mr Gerald Verney of the Hall has come back to Beckindale. I thought you'd like an item for your next issue.'

'An item . . . Saying what, exactly?'

'Well, his plans, like. Whether he intends to do any restoration . . . Whether he's going to have the Hunt there, start up the Hunt Ball again . . . what kind of activities his wife will take up. You know?'

'Mm . . .' The editor thought about it. Might not be bad, at that. 'You'll have to get a move on if it's to go in the next edition, Mr Brearley,' he said.

'I know that. I can do it this minute, if you like.'

'You can? Right, you're on. Four or five hundred words, say. Not more, we're a bit pressed for space this week.'

'Righto, then, Mr Towers. I'll get it to you by press time this evening.'

He put back the receiver, paused, went to the shelf and found the directories. He couldn't actually leave the Woolpack at the moment, for Henry was out – though he'd be back in a minute because he had the lunch to do. But you could interview a man by telephone, after all – at least you could get enough to make a piece for press time.

He happened to know the phone at the Hall had never been cut off because there had been the possibility of the local council using the building. He found the number and dialled.

Gerald Verney and his companion were going out of the front door when the phone rang. They gaped at each other. 'Are you expecting a call here, Rashley?' Gerald asked.

'No, I told them at the office to hold everything till I got back.' Rashley smiled across his plump face. 'Must be for you.'

'But who knows I'm here?'

'Oh, in a village, Mr Verney – everybody knows everything.'

With a shrug Verney went back and picked up the phone. 'Beckindale eight-one-two-eight,' he said, reading the number off the base of the instrument.

'Ah . . . er . . . Mr Verney?'

'Speaking.'

'Oh . . . er . . . Mr Verney, this is . . . er . . . the landlord of the local hostelry . . .' While he had been looking up the number and dialling, it had occurred to Amos that a speech of welcome could be delivered by telephone as well as in person. He'd put together a few resounding phrases, but they seemed to stick in his throat as he tried to utter them to this unseen presence at the Hall.

'Hello?' said Gerald with impatience. 'Hello, are you there?'

'Yes, I'm here, Mr Verney. Mr Verney, I want to wish you – '

'Would you speak up, please? I can't quite make out – '

'I was saying,' Amos said at the top of his voice, 'that I wanted to offer you the compliments of the locality.'

Gerald was holding the receiver away from his ear in dismay. The voice boomed on for another phrase or two. 'Hello?' it said, more subdued. 'Hello? Mr Verney?'

'Excuse me,' Gerald said, 'I'm rather pressed for time. Thank you for calling. Goodbye.' He put the phone back.

'Who was it?' Rashley said, coming back into the house from the porch.

'Heaven knows. Come on, let's get cracking. I'm getting hungry and we want to rough out the details of the advertisement about the sale before lunch.'

'Right, let's get going. But I wonder who could be taking the trouble to ring you the minute you stepped into the house?'

'Dunno,' Gerald Verney said. 'Some idiot.'

Chapter Two

Mr Towers of the *Hotten Courier* was considerably less than heart-broken when Amos rang, flustered, to say that he'd been to the Hall and found it empty. 'He's been there, but he's gone,' he reported on a mourning note. The editor made soothing noises but reflected he could use the space otherwise.

He had his reward for this calm good sense when his advertising manager rang through about an hour later. 'Hey, Bert, what d'you think?' he said. 'I've just received an advertisement from Fleck and Co. – box display, all that jazz. The Hall at Beckindale is going up for auction.'

'What?' cried Towers. 'Let's have a look at the copy.'

The advertising manager appeared within minutes. He laid a sheet of paper before Towers.

'The Hall, Miffield Rise, nr. Beckindale. This ten-bedroomed house built originally 1681, much improved,

21

set in its own grounds with stable block and outbuildings extending in all to eight acres excluding arable and pasture.

Together with contents, composed of furniture, silver and glass, porcelain, paintings, sculpture, objets d'art, rugs and carpets.

Fittings and appliances, tools, garden furniture, etc.

Farmland, including four farms under lease to well-established tenants. Grazing land let under short contracts. Woodland with hardwood trees, felling subject to Ministry approval.

Tarmacadamed drive and access roads to all areas of property.

The above property is to be sold by Public Auction at the above address on 30 July (unless previously sold) and on the two days following, with viewing for the three days prior to auction. For further details and full schedule of contents and viewing arrangements, please apply sole agents: Fleck and Co., High Street, Hotten.'

Mr Towers read this with his eyebrows rising higher and higher until they all but disappeared into his shaggy hairline. 'Wow,' he breathed. 'So that's why the heir turned up. To take a look before he put it under the hammer.'

'He's been there?'

'This very morning. Brearley rang in asking if I wanted an interview with him, but the bird had flown by the time he got his fountain pen unscrewed, I gather.'

'Oh,' said the advertising man, 'Mr Rashley of Fleck and Co., has just gone into the Six Bells with a stranger. I take it that's Mr Verney.'

Mr Towers, never one to stand on ceremony if he thought he could get a news item to interest his readers, grabbed up a notebook and ran from the room. He found Mr Rashley, whom he knew, sitting at lunch in the cosy dining-room of the Bells, opposite a tall and rather handsome man in a dark suit.

'Mr Verney?' Towers asked.

'Yes?' said the stranger, surprised.

Gerald Verney's surprise grew the more Towers questioned him. He couldn't understand why he should be an

22

object of interest to a local paper. He took refuge in that phrase, 'No comment,' but with that infallible human need to respond somehow when continually asked questions, he at last vouchsafed that he was selling the Hall because he couldn't afford to keep it. After that he applied himself to his stewed gooseberries and cream with so much concentration that Towers knew he was going to get nothing else, and withdrew.

To say that the Beckindalers were shocked next day when they saw the *Courier* is to understate by an astronomical figure. Sam Pearson bought the paper at the village shop on his morning walk, opened it casually as he turned in at the Emmerdale lane, and nearly had apoplexy.

'Annie! Annie!'

She ran out to meet him, scared by the strangled cry. She really expected to find him staggering, clutching his heart.

'Look at that,' he roared, thrusting the *Courier* at her.

At first she couldn't find what it was that had upset him – he'd crushed the paper in handing it to her half open. When she saw the advertisement, she frowned and sighed. 'So it's happened.'

'You mean you were expecting this?'

'Well, Dad, you know . . . Our own Mr Verney nearly sold the house a couple of times while he was still alive.'

'But that was just the *house*! For use as a college or summat. He had it on his conscious, probably – thinking of it standing empty, going to rack and ruin . . .'

Dolly was upstairs making the beds. She came hurrying down at the uproar. 'What's wrong?'

'Nowt to fret yourself about, lass,' Annie reassured her. 'The heir to the Verney Estate is selling it all.'

'Nowt to fret about?' cried Sam. 'The whole Verney Estate? Going, just like that?' He snapped his fingers. 'Wi' never a by your leave to us?'

'Now, Dad . . .'

'Don't "Now Dad" me! We're involved, aren't we? The man has no right to sell up and let who-knows-who buy into the district.'

'But he has the right, Mr Pearson,' Dolly put in in bewilderment. 'It's his land, isn't it?'

'Yes, but – '

23

'I mean, the house and the farms and the land and all that – he inherited them. I mean, only him. It's not like here at Emmerdale – it's not jointly owned?'

'Nay, but – '

'Dolly's right,' Annie said in a firm tone. 'It's no good harking back to the old days when the folk at the Hall felt a responsibility for Beckindale in general. Fact o't'matter is, this new lad has never seen us and doesn't know us – '

'And couldn't care less!'

'Well, be reasonable, Dad – why should he? From what we've heard, he's a Londoner, a businessman. I mean, not like Henry, this one's an office-business man. He probably wouldn't know where to start, managing the Miffield Estate with all its ramifications.'

'I don't mind him selling off bits o' Miffield Estate. After all, we bought Emmerdale from that. It's the Verney land – the Hall and the manor lands. Do you realize that the river and its banks above Beckindale are part of Miffield Estates? And the recreation ground?'

'Oh, come on – the parish council rents the recreation ground from Miffield Estates. Nobody's going to sell that away from us.'

'Don't you be too sure,' Sam groaned. 'Next thing we know, there'll be bungalows going up on the cricket pitch.'

Dolly giggled. 'Who'd want to build a bungalow on the cricket pitch?' she said. 'You know you're always saying yourself that it's at the back of beyond.'

'But there's folks like to buy bits at t'back of beyond and build bungalows on 'em,' Sam insisted. 'I tell thee, all the bits of Verney property we've been used to thinking of as belonging to t'village are going to be put back under "Miffield Estates" and we'll find ourselves losing everything.'

'Did you see Henry when you were in the shop?' Annie asked, worried despite herself by the picture he was painting.

'Nay, I were only in there a minute or so.'

'Happen we should ring him, ask if he's seen it.'

Henry had seen it. Amos had drawn his attention to it, forcibly. 'Mr Wilks!' he had exclaimed in a voice of horror. 'Look at that! Now you see what comes of not taking up Sam's idea of speaking a word or two to Mr Verney!'

'What?' Henry said, and read the advertisement over the marmalade jar where Amos was holding it out. The item surprised him a little but he refused to let it throw him. 'I hardly think the man made up his mind to sell just because he didn't find a welcoming committee on his doorstep, Amos.'

'It may well have influenced him. Any road, if you'd gone up to t'Hall, or let *me* –'

'But you did go, Amos.'

'Only when we'd closed up for the afternoon. I were obstructed in my duty as correspondent for the *Hotten Courier*.'

'Oh, the *Courier* has covered the news well enough,' Henry said. He'd found the little item about Mr Verney. 'Interviewed by our reporter in the restaurant of the Six Bells Inn, Mr Verney commented that financial pressures forced the sale of the fine old house. "I can't afford to keep it", he remarked.' Henry pointed the paragraph out to Amos. 'There, see?'

'Humph,' said Amos. 'Hardly does justice to the tragedy, does it?'

'Tragedy?'

'Well, I reckon most folk would say it's tragic. Fine old family reduced to penury . . .'

'Want to put a collecting box on the bar counter for them, then?' Henry enquired.

Nevertheless he understood the worry in Annie's manner when she rang him, and took himself off to the farm to have coffee and a chat with the others.

Sam had calmed down somewhat by then. He sat quiet, sipping his drink and listening while the others talked. The modern world of finance was beyond him; he felt he ought to try to learn a little.

'You see,' Henry said, 'the clue's in what Verney said to the reporter. He can't afford to keep the place. That's because of capital transfer tax.'

'But that's only a part of what he inherits,' Dolly said. 'I mean, all right, he's got to pay tax, but does that mean he has to sell up everything?'

Joe had been doing doodling sums on an old envelope. 'How big do you think the estate is?' he asked. 'I mean, not just Verney lands, the bits round here. I mean, the Miffield Estate, the company that managed the farms and that.'

'How big, Joe?' Henry enquired.

Joe made a tick against his sums. 'I reckon it's getting on for ten thousand acres.'

'What?' gasped Sam.

'Not far off, Grandad. Happen it's more. There's four farms rented out. One of 'em's about eight hundred acres, so let's say the others come to another two thousand. That's nigh on three thousand acres for a start. Then there's that grazing Clissold uses, and there must be more, to go by that advertising. So let's say another thousand. Then there's the woodland – you know, Verney Wood's a big place, and there's spinneys on Updale and near the Sleeve, the far side of the falls. I just did an adding-up and I reckon it's about ten thousand acres one way or t'other.'

'You could be right, lad,' Henry murmured.

'And what d'you think that's worth, at lowest estimate on today's prices?'

Henry paused with his hand over the biscuit tin. 'About... one million pounds.'

There was an audible in-drawing of breath. 'Never!' said Sam.

Matt cleared his throat. 'Reckon he's right, Grandad. Might even be more.'

'Well, then!' cried Dolly. 'What's he selling up for? And all this talk of not being able to afford to keep the Hall? He's worth at least a million!'

'Yes, but –' Annie began.

'Yes, but,' agreed her son. 'Any idea what the capital transfer tax is?'

Everyone except Henry looked blank. Henry said, 'Sixty per cent.'

'You what?' gasped Matt. 'Sixty per cent?'

'Six . . . hundred . . . thousand . . . pounds,' Joe said, spelling it out.

There was a shattered silence, broken by Annie who got up and said, 'More coffee?'

'I reckon I need it after that,' Matt said. 'This feller's got to pay over six hundred thousand pounds?'

'Yes. Just because he inherited the Verney name and

26

estates. And of course he hasn't got six hundred thousand pounds.'

'Who has?' wondered Dolly.

'So he's got to sell.'

'But . . . couldn't he . . . I mean, I've read about it,' Dolly said. 'You hand over your house to the government in lieu of death duties.'

Henry shook his head. 'The government doesn't want any more stately homes,' he said. 'They cost a lot to keep up – unless you leave the income for the upkeep it's just not on. You have to sell and hand over the money instead.'

'And besides,' Joe put in, 'there's nothing very stately about the Hall. It's a nice old place, but it's had bits added on and taken off.'

'That's true,' his grandfather agreed. 'I remember during t'War, old Mr Verney pulled down the conservatory and a passage that led to it, because he needed the glass for cloches. And then when you could get building materials again just after War, he built on that garage with the room above it.'

'Yes, you see, it's just an ordinary house though it happens to have been built originally in the seventeen hundreds. You can tell it's not up to much because nobody seemed to want it when George Verney tried to sell it or rent it after he left.'

'So the only way Gerald Verney's going to raise the six hundred thousand pounds the tax man wants is by selling up entirely. It's the land that'll raise the money.'

'Oh, I don't know so much,' Annie said, recalling visits to the Hall in days gone by. 'Some of the things there are beautiful.'

'Such as what?' Henry asked, recalling two visits he'd made before George Verney left. He had a different standpoint from Annie. He liked good silver and handsome furniture, but he knew that pleasant things weren't necessarily valuable.

Annie talked about gilt tables and Dresden ornaments. 'Aye,' Henry agreed, 'they'll fetch a bit, no doubt. But . . . well, you see, Annie, you can buy an ormolu table for a couple of hundred pounds. That's not chicken feed to us, but it's not going to help reach a target like six hundred thousand.'

'You know,' Sam said suddenly, 'there was something up

27

at t'Hall that was tremendously valuable.'

'What?'

'Can't recall! You remember me speaking of old Ethel Verney, Annie?'

'Who? No, I – wait a minute. You mean the spinster sister?'

'That's the one. Sister to Mr Oswald. Now let me see . . . It was Mr Oswald fought in t'Boer War, and *his* father were in t'Crimea – is that right, Annie?'

'I've no idea,' she said. 'Is it important?'

'Well, one on 'em – dashed if I can recall which – went for a long holiday on t'Continent. They used to do that in them days. Went to Rome, and Paris, and Biarritz, and Baden-Baden . . . It must ha' been Mr Oswald's father, I think. That's right! Miss Ethel, she said to me one day – '

'You used to hobnob wi' her, did you, Grandad?'

'Don't thee be so cheeky, young Joe. She talked to me – why shouldn't she? A real nice old lady, were Miss Ethel. She used to drive around in a little dogcart, and when I put the pony to, or took it out, she'd pass time of day wi' me. And one day when Mr Oswald had told her he wouldn't buy her a new carriage though t'old one were getting shaky, she said summat to me.'

By this time almost everyone had lost interest in the tale. Dolly was putting milk and sugar in Matt's second cup of coffee, Joe had gone back to his addition sums, Henry was re-reading the advertisement in the *Courier*.

Unaware, Sam went on with his memories: 'She said to me, did Miss Ethel, "I've a good mind to order a brougham and show him I've a mind of my own." And I said, "Where'd you get the money, Miss Ethel?" – for in them days, y'see, ladies had to ask their menfolk for every penny almost. And she said, "Oh, I could walk into the house and walk out again with a fortune in my hands if I'd a mind to, Sam." She allus called me Sam. Nice old lady. Hundreds came to her funeral. I were eighteen, I mind – got my first proper suit to go to Miss Ethel's funeral . . .' Sam glanced about. No one seemed to be paying much attention. 'So you see,' he remarked, louder, 'happen there's something in the contents of the house that'd pay off the death duties.'

'What, six hundred thousand pounds' worth?' scoffed Joe.

28

'Besides, Grandad,' Matt put in, 'sixty per cent of whatever's in the house – what it's worth, I mean – goes to the tax.'

'Not necessarily,' Henry said. 'I mean, it depends.'

'On what?'

'Well, the fact that the date of the sale is fixed means that the estate has been valued for probate. That would include the house and contents. The tax is calculated on that. It's a once and for all calculation.'

'You mean that if something valued at ten pounds was really worth a hundred, it'd still only have a ten pound value for death duties?'

'If that's what the probate figure showed.'

'Hey, up,' teased Joe, 'mebbe that fairytale you were telling us was true, Grandad. And if it was, and there was something in the house Miss Ethel knew about but her brother didn't, happen it's still there – a nice little windfall for Gerald Verney.'

Gerald Verney felt he could do with all the windfalls he could find. True enough, he was going to come into money even after the capital transfer tax was paid. But there were bequests to other members of the family to be taken out of the balance, and legal expenses and one thing and another. He certainly wasn't going to lose by the sale of the Verney estates, but he wasn't going to be a millionaire either.

And the fact was, his own business wasn't doing any too well. He had bought a share in it by invitation, and for a time had made a more than reasonable income from it, but trading conditions had changed a lot.

Gerald was the son of the elder Gerald Verney, brother to the owner of the Hall. After service in World War Two, this younger Verney had been unable to settle down to civilian life. During his wartime career in the Navy the elder Gerald had got to know the Mediterranean, so when post-war Britain became just too irksome he emigrated to Rome with his wife and small son. His ambition was to train for opera. He had a fine baritone voice, and the death of his father had given him just sufficient money to pay for lessons and live in a wing of an old villa near Ostia.

The young Gerald had been sent home to school in

England at the expense of the head of the family, George Verney of the Hall. He had then gone on to Cambridge. He had never really enjoyed the faintly Bohemian existence of his parents in their seedy, crumbling apartment in Italy, nor had he felt any pride in his father's operatic career – which, to say the least, was limited.

The elder Gerald died of, sad to say, a virus that lurked in some corner of the dingy old villa. The young Gerald thus inherited a small sum of money which he invested in the import-export business because he didn't want to risk it in any high-flying venture. A friend in Rome who had contacts throughout the Mediterranean in the oil and resin business recommended Precosolv as sound. But there had been war in Lebanon, revolution in Libya, trouble in Turkey . . . times were hard. It would be nice to have some substantial sum through the sale of the Verney Estate so that he didn't need to worry any more about the volatile politics of the countries that produced cosmetic oils.

One good thing had come from his father's life in Italy; from time to time visitors used to turn up at the Hall with a letter of introduction to George Verney from the elder Gerald: 'Signor Marducco is a neighbour of mine, please give him a bed for a night or two' or something of that kind. Sometimes they dropped in on Gerald in London too. Even after his father died, they still kept up contacts. He felt he ought to write to one or two of them, to let them know what had recently happened: that his uncle was gone, and the house in Beckindale would soon be gone too so that they mustn't rely on being able to tour Britain and drop in at the Hall for hospitality.

Gerald's wife Charlotte hadn't yet seen the Hall. She had visited Uncle George, of course, but only in his place in Cannes. 'I suppose I ought to take a look, darling,' she said. 'Just in case I might take a fancy to it and want to live there.'

'For Pete's sake, don't,' he implored. 'It's not a bad old house, but it would cost a mint to renovate. Still . . .' he sighed, 'the views are superb. When I was a kid I used to stand and stare out over the moors and think they went on to the end of the world.'

'We have to be up there for the sale, Gerry,' she pointed out. 'We may as well go a bit early and take a look.'

'But we can't *stay* in the house, you know. All the furniture's been grouped and labelled for sale.'

'But there is a hotel or something?'

'Not in the village, as far as I recall. While I was up there seeing Rashley, I stayed at quite a decent place called the Feathers, in Connelton. That's an easy drive from Beckindale.'

'Ring them, darling, will you? You'd better book from . . . when's the sale?'

'30 July.'

'Well, then, we'd better go next week and stay a fortnight. You could say it's in lieu of a summer hol!'

Holidaymakers did find their way to Beckindale, but not in very large numbers. However, the locals did actually notice an increase in the number of visitors. Many of them drove around with sketch maps, taking up a stance on high points to look at the farms which were up for sale.

'They seem a bit stony-faced, some of them,' Matt remarked to Joe.

'Well, they're looking at the land as an investment, I s'pose.'

'It'd be better if the tenants could buy out their freeholds.'

'Depends. Maddocks won't want to, for instance. He's getting on, and his son's gone to Texas or somewhere to work in computers.'

'Aye, that's right. He won't want his freehold. So I suppose that's one farm that might go to a syndicate.'

'Seems to me, hardly anybody's got the money to buy a farm and start out on his own these days.' Joe hesitated. 'Ever think of going out for yourself, Matt?'

Matt shook his head. 'Emmerdale's good enough for me,' he said. Then, with a question in his eyes, 'So long as you're happy with the arrangement.'

'Oh, *I'm* happy,' Joe assured him. 'It's only . . .'

'What?'

'I just wondered . . . Does Dolly ever talk about a place of your own?'

'Oh aye. Some time in the future, of course.'

'Mm . . .' said Joe.

31

Matt studied him. 'She said anything to you, then?'

'No. Not a word. But I thought she seemed . . .'

'Seemed what?'

'Restless.'

'Nay, she hasn't settled down at Emmerdale properly yet. It's only been a couple of months.'

'I suppose that's what it is.' They were finishing the afternoon milking. They completed their work in silence, but Matt was thoughtful.

After tea he suggested a walk to Dolly. The long summer evening stretched ahead of them. At the moment there was a slight lull in farming activity – hay and silage had been made, barley and wheat weren't quite right for cutting yet. Across the dale on a distant field a tractor was busy on a second hay crop, its engine like the drone of some giant insect. Dog-roses were out in the hedgerows, their faint sweet scent reminding Dolly of apple peel.

They strolled hand in hand down to the village then on up the lane, hardly taking note of their steps. Matt was trying to think of a way to ask Dolly if she was happy at Emmerdale. To him it seemed an odd thing to be asking. If she weren't, she'd tell him, surely?

Matt himself was so straightforward and uncomplicated that he couldn't even picture Dolly's state of mind. She loved him, he was sure of that. She had told him so. When he asked her to marry him, he'd explained his role as partner in Emmerdale Farm. She knew all about his financial status. This being so, she surely understood that his home was Emmerdale. How could she be 'restless'?

'You know, Dolly,' he began, 'that six thousand pounds that came to me just afore we got married?'

'Yes,' she said absently, tweaking a leaf from the hedge as they walked, 'what about it?'

'It's in t'building society.'

'Aye, of course.'

'How would you feel about taking it out and putting it as a deposit on a house?'

There was a pause. Then, with a reaction that astounded him, she flung her arms round him and hugged him hard. When she let him go, he saw tears glinting in her eyes.

'Eh, love, what's up?' he asked, with his arm around her

shoulders. 'I thought it might make you happy if I put the idea up.'

'Oh, Matt, it does, it does!' she whispered. 'I'd just love to have a little house of our own.'

'You would?' He was perplexed, but luckily Dolly was so taken up with this new, wonderful idea that she didn't notice.

Dolly often scolded herself for being discontented at Emmerdale. She was married to the most wonderful man in the world, and living with a family who were kindness itself. What did it matter if she were gently scolded for picking the sweet peas, or directed to go and amuse herself so that Annie could get on with the washing?

Dolly wanted to play her part in the household. She was trying to learn how to take part in the milking schedule, but it would be a long time before she could be really useful. However, in the house, she felt she had more to offer. She was quite a good cook and a passable needlewoman. But the fact of the matter was, Annie was better at everything than Dolly. Not that she threw her weight about – nothing could be further from the truth. It was just that it seemed pointless for Dolly to get in the way when Annie could do everything so much more quickly and effectively.

The worst things for Dolly were the early mornings and the evenings. She felt it was her duty as a wife to be up and making Matt's early tea for him, and then to get his breakfast ready when he came back from morning milking. But she had never been good at early rising, and she had to admit that Annie was. Dolly felt guilty at being so heavy-eyed and slow-witted when Annie was grilling bacon, making tea, stirring porridge, buttering toast, all at the same time. Dolly had come to terms with it. She sat down with the others to the breakfast table, having contributed by staying out of Annie's way.

The evenings were more difficult. Dolly longed to have time to spend alone with Matt. Oh, of course, she could ask to use the front room – but how embarrassing that was, to have to say, 'You won't mind, Annie, if we have the evening alone together?' And come the winter, she'd have to have the electric fire on a bit in advance, which meant making up your mind beforehand whether you wanted to sit there. Besides, that was the whole point – you couldn't just please yourself.

Dolly longed to be able to sit across the tea table from Matt, speaking or not speaking just as they wished, holding hands afterwards as they watched television or listened to the radio.

At the moment it was simple enough to be alone – they could go out for a walk. But even that made Dolly feel guilty. Matt had done a long, hard day. It seemed wrong to drag him out to trudge round a village he already knew well enough. Besides, when the good weather ended, there would be no attraction in going out into the dark and cold.

Now here was Matt himself putting up the notion that they should get a home of their own. Dolly herself would never have suggested it. It would have sounded ungrateful and selfish to want to move from Emmerdale. But if Matt had it in his own mind, then it was all right – she could admit she longed to be away from the family, in their own little world, just like other newly-weds.

She began to sketch out the kind of place she thought they could afford. Sure enough, Matt's six thousand pounds wouldn't get them a palace – but Dolly didn't want a palace.

Just about that moment, they turned a corner in the lane that was known as Miffield Rise, and there, gleaming in the dusk, was the gatehouse of the Verney grounds. It was a pretty little lodge, once just a little square stone cottage but refurbished in the early Victorian era by the Verney who had made the Grand Tour and come back with ideas on art and architecture. It now had a facing of smooth stone, a bay with arched windows facing towards the unused gates, and a little ornamental porch over the door. It was only one storey, and to the outward view seemed to have two rooms at the front and two at the back.

'There!' Dolly said. 'Now that's the sort of place . . .'

'The porter's lodge?'

'Why not? It's empty, isn't it? Been empty ever since Mr Verney went away, from what I can gather. It must be for sale. Everything else is.'

They walked through the open gates and peered in at the windows, but darkness was gathering and it was impossible to see anything inside.

'It's solid enough,' Dolly said, touching the stonework.

'Need a heck of a lot done to it, love.'

'But we could do it gradual, Matt?'

She had turned towards him, and though he couldn't make out her expression there was eagerness in every line of her body. He smoothed her soft fair hair back from her brow and dropped a kiss on it.

'We don't even know if it's for sale separate or as part of the house and grounds.'

'We could find out, eh?'

'Oh, aye, no problem. Henry's got the sale catalogue and details.'

'Shall's go and ask him then, Matt?'

'What, now?'

'No time like the present.'

'Ye-es . . . well . . . not a bad idea to drop in at t'Woolpack for a drink before we head for home. All right, then, let's do that.'

The quickest way back to the village was down the lane a little and then by a footpath round the side of Verney Woods which would bring them out on the slope above the houses. They walked along without haste, pausing now and then to steal a kiss. They were moving from the shadows of the woods to the sloping meadows when Matt's attention was attracted by something gleaming white in the twilight.

'What's that?' he muttered, stopping.

'What, Matt?'

'On Top Twenty field . . .' He hopped over the wall and walked forward. He put out his hand. It met a wooden post.

A post? Three feet in from the dyke of the field? Who on earth would waste his time driving a post into a field?.

But even more odd, there was another about three feet further on, and then another. But then they came to an end.

He turned and went back to Dolly. 'That's right queer,' he said.

'What is?'

'Three posts stuck in the ground.'

'Kids, was it?'

'But what for? Any road, they feel as if they've been driven in with a sledge hammer – firm as a rock.'

'I expect Joe did it.'

'But what for? Three posts, and then nowt. He never mentioned it to me . . .'

'Well, we'll ask him in the morning. Come on,

Woolpack'll be putting up t'shutters!'

He nodded and took her arm. They made their way down the meadow to the next field and then into Beckindale. But before Matt went with Dolly into the path leading to the inn, he returned back for one more look at the posts.

There they were, faintly gleaming in the fading light. There was something strange about them, almost threatening.

Chapter Three

Henry handed over the catalogue of the Verney sale with the quip: 'Going to buy the mahogany chiffonier?'

'What on earth's a chiffonier?'

'No idea. We'll see when the viewing days come on.'

Matt flicked through the pages as he waited for Henry to bring the drinks he'd ordered. The information about the land and buildings was on a separate schedule. He tucked it all back together again and put it under his arm to pick up the sherry and the half of bitter. He turned back as he was about to go.

'Henry,' he said, 'did Joe say owt to you about putting posts in Top Twenty?'

Henry was already on his way to serve another customer. He said over his shoulder: 'Posts?'

'Three white posts. In Top Twenty field.'

'Top Twenty? Up the slope, next the wood?'

'Aye. Did Joe mention it?' It was clear Henry knew nothing about it. 'Never mind, then. It's kids playing around, I suppose.'

Henry nodded and let it drop. He had other things on his mind. He and Amos were engaged in guerrilla warfare at the moment, and he couldn't see any way of bringing it to an end without open hostility.

'Look, Amos, it'll only be a few days. Marion says in her letter, three or four days.'

'That's as may be, Mr Wilks,' Amos said with an audible sigh. 'But I thought it was agreed that we didn't take paying guests?'

'This isn't quite like that, Amos. It's a friend of Marion's. You couldn't expect me to say no when my own daughter asks me to put a friend up.'

'Humph,' said Amos. 'We don't even know whether this feller can speak English.'

'Must do,' Henry said. 'He wouldn't be travelling in the north of England if he couldn't make himself understood.'

'Well, though I handled Italian POWs in North Africa, I never learned more than a couple of words of Eytie, so it's up to you, Mr Wilks. If he needs an interpreter, happen you'll take it on.'

Henry didn't speak more than a couple of words either, though he'd visited Marion in Rome. He didn't much fancy having to convey the subtleties of Yorkshire life to a volatile Roman. Truth to tell, he was perplexed about the whole thing. All of a sudden this chap was going to turn up in Beckindale and stay a few days. What on earth for? What could there be in Beckindale to attract a bloke from Rome?

The first surprise occurred next day when the visitor arrived in a little hired Fiat. The guest, airily referred to in Marion's PS to her letter as 'my friend Frankie,' turned out to be one Francesca Zorelli, a voluptuous young lady with chestnut hair and great dark eyes. 'Everyone calls me Frankie,' she explained when the two men had closed their gaping mouths and were trying to explain they'd expected a man. 'But it's better, no? Already there are two men here – it's nice for you to have a woman guest, to make a little change.'

'Oh, quite,' Henry said in a faint voice. Amos was making sounds that came out like 'Ug-ug-ug' but luckily didn't emerge as protests. Amos was dead against having 'female persons' staying in the Woolpack, and as to Italian female persons – !

'Now look, there's nothing to do but grin and bear it,' Henry said when he'd shown the guest to her room and left her to unpack. To be candid, Henry was already grinning. The whole thing struck him as irresistibly comic. It was lucky Marion hadn't said more in her letter. If it had been clear that her friend was a girl, nothing would have induced Amos to agree to receiving her at the Woolpack.

'What are people going to say?' moaned Amos. 'A strange

young woman – !'

'Nowt strange about her. Quite the contrary: she had all the usual female appearance only more so.'

'That's what I mean!' cried Amos. 'She's . . . she's . . .'

'Sexy?'

'Mr Wilks!' It was a cry of horror.

'All right, Amos. We'll take a vow of chastity.'

'Mr Wilks, I will not have that kind of language in this establishment!'

Henry made himself straighten his features into a serious expression. 'Righto, Amos. We'll be calm and controlled about this.'

'I always am controlled, and I'm not going to change now. All I want to say is that I never asked this young woman here, I allow her to stay under protest, and if something bad comes of it, on your head be it!'

With this awful proclamation of doom, Amos resigned himself to the torture of the next few days. He was going to have his household upset by a talkative foreign lady, he was going to find nylon tights drying in the bathroom, he was going to have his leg pulled by the regulars. So be it. He had lived through worse. Not *much* worse, but still, he had survived.

The object of his suspicions was upstairs in the guest room consulting a tourist map of the district. It was the largest scale map she'd been able to get but even so, Verney Hall wasn't marked on it. She already had a copy of the announcement of the sale in her handbag, but she needed a sale catalogue. She could get that in Hotten; she'd seen signposts for Hotten as she drove north from London to Beckindale.

She went downstairs. 'My room is charming,' she remarked. 'Tell me, what time do you serve lunch?'

'Serve lunch?' Amos echoed, appalled.

'Where is the dining-room? It would be good to eat early, I think, and then to go exploring.'

'I . . . er . . . we . . . er . . . You're under a misapprehension, miss,' Amos said. 'This isn't a hotel. We don't have a dining-room. We don't serve lunch.'

'No lunch?' She looked at him with round eyes.

'I'm sorry, Miss Zorelli – '

'Call me Frankie.'

'I'm sorry, Frankie, my daughter doesn't seem to have made it clear to you,' said Henry. 'This is a pub. You know the English word "pub"?'

'Of course. *Molto simpático*, the pub.'

'Well, *simpático* or not, most pubs don't have a restaurant. Some serve lunch – bar snacks.'

'Snacks?'

'Bread and cheese, ham sandwich . . .'

'Oh, I see. Well, the sandveech will be quite satisfactory to me. Also coffee. And then I go and take a view of the district, and perhaps go to 'Otten. 'Otten is not far?'

Amos glared at Henry and Henry looked at Amos. He shrugged. What was the use? All right, just this once. 'I'll make you a sandwich and a cup of coffee, Miss Zorelli.'

'Frankie.'

'But I'm afraid I'll have to make it clear that we don't serve meals. My partner and I cook our own meals but – '

'Oh, then that is even better. I will have whatever you are having, of course, for this evening. But at the moment I am quite eager to get out to look at the countryside so if you please – the sandveech?'

Henry drew in a breath. Then his good humour reasserted itself. 'Certainly, *signorina*,' he said. 'With or without mustard?'

He made enough coffee for the three of them. Amos took his out to the bar, saying he had chores to do. His back was stiff with disapproval. Henry sat down to chat with Frankie.

'What exactly brought you to Beckindale?' he enquired. 'It seems an unlikely choice for a holiday if you come from Rome?'

'Not at all,' she protested. 'As it happens, I have friends in Rome who used to visit here in times gone by. You perhaps know that there was a singer who sometimes appeared in the chorus of the opera – Gerrardo Verni.'

'By heck!' cried Henry. 'Gerald Verney? I did hear that the father of the present Gerald had lived in Rome.'

'Era lui,' agreed Frankie, munching the sandwich of thick ham and brown bread. She had approached it with some apprehension but to her surprise it was good. So was the coffee. It wouldn't be too uncomfortable after all, and it was

39

going to be worth it . . .

'You knew Gerald Verney?'

'No, no, not I. But I have a friend who knew him very well, and visited at the villa.'

'The Hall, it's called.'

'The 'All.' She hesitated. 'That is not on my map, the 'All.'

'It isn't? No, it'd only be on a very large-scale map. It's no kind of a tourist attraction, not like Rievaulx Abbey or the like. Well, fancy you knowing about the Hall. Too bad it's empty these days. You could have dropped in and talked about old acquaintances.'

'I should quite like to see it, nevertheless, Signor Veelks.' She wrinkled her nose. 'An impossible name for me to say. May I call you Henry?' She pronounced it 'Enry. It sounded rather odd. But her smile was winning. Henry nodded.

'What do you do, Frankie? You a singer too?'

'Not at all! No, I have a leetle business of my own.'

'Oh, you do? What kind of business?'

'I buy things.'

'What sort of things?'

'Whatever I think will sell.'

'Ah, you buy and sell?'

'*Si, si.*'

'You have a boutique or something?'

'No, nothing like that. Well, Henry, your sandveech was delicious. And now I must go. Tell me, which road takes me out of the village towards 'Otten?'

Henry gave her directions. He came out to see her drive off the way he had pointed. As he came back through the bar Amos was on his hands and knees with a dustpan and brush. He had heard all that was said.

'She seems a very nice girl,' Henry said, pausing close by. 'You should have joined us in the kitchen, Amos.'

Amos swept a recalcitrant thread into the dustpan. 'You mark my words, Mr Wilks,' he said, 'that one is up to no good.'

'Amos!'

'She's a "friend of a friend of the late Gerald Verney". You're not telling me that's a good reason for visiting Beckindale?'

'Eeh, lad, you'd be suspicious if t'Queen herself paid us a visit.'

But all the same, the words stayed in his mind. What could have brought her to Beckindale? Amos was right, there was scant reason to come even though she had a friend who used to know the father of the present owner.

The object of his thoughts drove out of the village and up the slowly climbing road that took her updale towards Hotten. On the far side of the little river she could see men working in a field. They weren't harvesting grass, as she'd seen in other fields en route to Beckindale. They seemed to be digging or hammering. But agriculture wasn't her speciality. She paid no heed and turned at the corner towards the market town.

The men in the field were putting in white posts. Joe Sugden was amazed when he came out of the footpath through the woods and found it to be true. He looked back over his shoulder at Matt. 'By heck!' he said.

Matt came to join him. He too was startled. 'They've put in more since last night,' he said. 'What the dickens are they up to?'

'God knows, but I'm going to find out!' Joe was furious. He strode down the field towards them. He wished now he'd come by the road, on the tractor, and driven into the field by the field gate. He could have driven the machine over those posts and demolished them in ten seconds flat. But because Matt had told the story of seeing the posts from the footpath, Joe had taken the same route – little expecting to find a team of three men at work here.

'What do you think you're doing?' he shouted as they drew near.

The oldest man looked up. 'Should be obvious,' he said.

'You've no right here! You get those posts out and be off!'

He stared at Joe. 'And who might you be?'

'I'm the owner of this land!'

The other two had stopped in their work, sledge hammers resting on the ground. By their side was a pile of stakes painted white.

'What's your name?' asked the foreman.

'Sugden, Joe Sugden. And this is part of Emmerdale Farm.'

'Emmerdale Farm?' He produced a folded paper from his breast pocket, much creased and worn at the corners. It was a photocopy of a ground plan. He stared at it for a moment then folded it up again and returned it to his pocket. He shrugged. 'I'm only carrying out instructions,' he said.

'Instructions? Whose instructions?'

'Mr Rashley's.'

At the name, Joe stiffened. He felt as if a bucket of cold water had been thrown in his face. Mr Rashley was the manager of Fleck and Co., the estate agent and valuer handling the Verney sale.

'Mr Rashley's got nowt to do wi' our property,' he said. 'You clear off back to Hotten, and tell him to keep off Emmerdale land.'

'Hmm,' the foreman said in embarrassment. 'We were told to get these posts up today at latest, because of the viewing.'

'Viewing?'

'Of the Verney Estate.'

'But this isn't part of the Verney Estate!'

'So you say, chum.' The man was clearly at a loss. 'But according to this sketch map, the line of posts goes here to mark the edge of Verney land.'

'But this is our twenty-acre field!'

'I think you're wrong.'

'Wrong? Good God, man, we just finished taking hay off it! Go and look in the Dutch barn if you doubt it!'

'Look, I don't know anything about hay. All I know is that my instructions from Mr Rashley are to get these posts in, and I've got to do it.'

'You don't put another post in this field, lad, and don't think it.' Joe was white with anger, his eyes sparkling with disbelieving indignation. 'It's a mistake, some office botch-up. You get back to Hotten and tell 'em we're not having strangers tramping over our Top Twenty field hammering stakes in. I can see it's a genuine mistake but you tell Rashley if he sends anybody else to muck about here, I'll have the law on him.'

There was a hesitation. Then the other turned to his workers. 'All right, lads. Pack up for the moment. We'd best get back to Hotten to ask what's to do.'

Joe and Matt watched in angry silence while they bundled up their staves and the coil of thick string, hefted their hammers on their shoulders, and trooped off to the road where a little open truck awaited them. They clambered in and drove away.

'Would you credit it?' Joe muttered.

'It's funny, that,' Matt said. 'I thought so last night when me and Dolly first saw it.'

'I don't think it's funny,' Joe said. 'I think it's a liberty, and I'm going to give Rashley a piece of my mind before the day's out.'

'D'you think we ought to tell Henry first?'

'No, what the dickens do we need Henry for?' But then Joe paused. 'Happen we'd better,' he said. 'There's some kind of a mix-up, and Henry's good at disentangling things. Come on, we'd best get to the phone.'

Henry could tell by Joe's manner that something bad had occurred. 'What's up, lad?'

'I don't want to talk about it on the phone, Henry. Can you come to the farm?'

'What, now?'

'The sooner the better.'

'I'm on my way.'

Dolly was in Hotten enquiring whether the gatehouse of the Hall was open to separate offer. Annie had been busy on a morning's baking but had suspended her activities at Joe's news. Her father was gardening, but came in when he saw Henry drive up.

'You're too late, Henry we've had us elevenses,' he teased.

'Aye, and I've had mine – with a charming Italian lady.'

'An Italian?'

'A friend of Marion's. Joe and Matt inside?'

'Aye, they came in a while gone.' Sam eyed him. 'Summat wrong, Henry?'

'Seems so. Joe rang me, seemed in a bit of a tizz.'

Sam decided to give up his struggle with the blackfly on the broad beans and come indoors to hear what was going on. He'd heard Matt's story of the three white posts in the Top Twenty at breakfast time, but hadn't attached too much importance to it. Now, as he listened to the rest, a pang of anxiety began to gnaw him.

'You mean they were there on our property hammering fence-posts in?' Henry demanded, amazed.

'I tell you, Henry, they seemed absolutely sure of

themselves. The foreman had a map.'

'Map?'

'Sheet of paper, sketch map. I suppose,' Matt put in, 'Mr Rashley must have supplied him with that.'

'But that's incredible,' Henry cried. 'Rashley's a sensible, intelligent man. Fleck and Co. are a well-established firm.'

'Henry,' Annie began.

'What did they say, exactly, Joe?'

'I don't recall, *exactly*. They said Mr Rashley had sent them to get the posts in by today because of the viewing for the sale, and when I asked them what the dickens they wanted with a bit of Emmerdale, they said it were Verney's land.'

'It's just a mistake,' Annie said. 'We've been farming that land for years.'

'All my life, so far as I can recall,' Joe said. 'It's not Verney's land.'

'Wait a bit,' said Sam.

'Wait a bit? Nowt o't'sort! I'm going to Hotten and tell Mr Rashley to mind what he's about. I want you to come with me, Henry.'

'No, I didn't mean that. I meant, stop talking, I'm trying to remember summat. What was that you said?'

'About what?'

'You said they told you it were "Verney's land"?'

'Aye, but of course they would say that, seeing –'

'You know,' Sam said in a stifled voice, 'that was what your Jacob used to call it, Annie.'

'What?'

'That field. He allus referred to it as "Verney's Land".'

All eyes turned on Annie. She shook her head, her grey eyes looking back into the past. She couldn't remember her husband using that phrase. 'It's always just been Top Twenty – the twenty-acre field.'

'Same here,' Joe said. 'I never remember hearing Dad call it "Verney's Land".' But he was watching his grandfather with troubled eyes. Sam had a good memory for things of the past. 'We've always farmed that land,' he went on stoutly. 'I remember the first time I was allowed to help with stooking barley – that were on Top Twenty.'

'Nay,' Sam said, 'we haven't allus farmed that land. It

44

were waste land originally.'

Annie shook her head again, trying to recall the days of her youth when she first came to Emmerdale as a bride. Jacob had just been demobbed from the Navy, was full of good intentions about making the farm a model business. It was a fact that he had made a lot of changes then, in face of quite a lot of opposition from his father.

'I can remember Jacob saying to me that it were a pity to let that land go to waste,' murmured Sam.

'But Top Twenty were never waste land. It's always been in use.'

'Nay, lad, this were afore you were born. That stretch had nowt growing on it but nettles and thistles.'

'What, you mean the whole of that meadow, between the woods and the lane, were just . . .'

'Rough ground. Brambles on it, I remember. The kids used to go in there and get jam jars full for their mothers to make bramble jelly. All the walls were down on the road side.'

Annie made a slight movement. 'I remember the brambles,' she said with a troubled frown. 'Jack gathered a whole basinful . . .'

'Jacob went walking across it,' Sam continued. 'It were a rainy day, I recall. He came back soaked. Don't you recall, Annie, that winter when he had so many big ideas? He took his tools and he started on them walls.'

'Aye,' she murmured. 'I remember he went mending walls. Were that Top Twenty?'

There was no reply for a moment. The old man was lost in memories.

'Go on, Sam,' Wilks said with an anxious look at Joe.

'Nowt much else, really. He mended t'walls on lane end, opened t'wall between that piece and Emmerdale land, and let the cows through to graze t'lower slope while he got the brambles off the top end o' the meadow. Following year, he put it to grass, if I'm right. After that, he put it into rotation.'

'But Sam,' groaned Henry, 'he couldn't just take somebody else's land?'

'I'm just telling you what I remember, lad.'

'And what was old Mr Verney doing all this while?' Joe burst out. 'Standing by letting it happen?'

'Don't seem likely,' Matt said.

Annie got up suddenly and went to take her bread out of the oven. The fragrance of the new loaves flooded the kitchen. She knocked the baking tins on the edge of the table then tipped the bread on a wire tray to cool. It seemed a normal, everyday act in the midst of this strange unreal tale.

'Which Mr Verney are we talking about?' Henry appealed. 'The George Verney I knew?'

'Nay, his father. He were George Verney too, but different stuff to his son. A real old tartar – fair, mind, but tough.'

'And he let Annie's husband take over twenty acres of his land without lifting a finger?'

Sam hunched his shoulders and let them drop. 'I dunno,' he said. 'I'm just telling you what I remember. I'm right, aren't I, Annie? Jacob enclosed that bit o' land on the lane side and opened it on Emmerdale side so that it became part of Emmerdale.'

'By heck,' Joe said flatly.

Annie looked at the other loaves in the oven, took off her oven gloves, and sat down again. 'I think Dad's right. I think that field had something done to it by Jacob. I don't know the ins and outs of it because he never talked about it to me.'

'Not to me neither,' Sam said.

'So what's the situation now?' Joe muttered.

'Well . . . if it's been Emmerdale land for so long, happen it belongs. By usage, or some such term.'

'Usage?'

'Sort of like squatters' rights?' Matt put in.

'We've never squatted at Emmerdale!' Sam cried. 'Don't ever use such a word to me!'

'Nay, but Sam, Matt's in the right of it. If we've had the use of that bit of ground for twenty-five years without protest from Verneys, then happen we're the rightful owners by some such right.'

'Who would know?' Matt wondered.

'Dunno. It's a thing for a lawyer, is this,' Henry said. 'Can I use your phone, Annie?'

He had just finished making an appointment to see their man of business in Hotten when Dolly came in from her trip there. She stopped short at the looks on their faces. 'What's wrong?' she asked in dismay.

'Nothing much, happen,' Matt said reassuringly. 'I'll tell you all about it by and by. Did you see them about the gatehouse?'

'Aye, and they say it might be possible to put it up as a separate lot in the auction. We're to go in and discuss it with him as soon as possible. I said you'd ring and make an appointment. Was that all right?'

Matt coloured a little with embarrassment. 'Going to look a bit funny, isn't it?' he said. 'Talking to Rashley about us buying a house from Verney's when on t'other hand we're accusing him of trying to make off with some Emmerdale land?'

'What?' asked Dolly, bemused.

'It's complicated, love. Listen, Henry, if you're going to Hotten later, happen I could go in with you.'

'Righto. What house is this, then, Dolly?' Henry said, willing to turn his attention to other, less dire matters.

'That little lodge at the gates of Verney's grounds. It is for sale, but they hadn't thought of selling it separate. It's awfully nice in Fleck and Co.'s office,' she went on. 'Old-fashioned and leather-upholstered, you know? And what do you think? While I was there, an Italian lady came in!'

'What?' cried Henry, turning back as he was about to go out.

'Ever so smart. Gucci shoes, I should think, and a handbag to match.'

'Did she happen to say her name?'

'No,' Dolly replied, surprised. 'She just bought a sale catalogue and went out.'

'A sale catalogue? For Verney's sale?'

Dolly nodded, looking at him with wide eyes. Why should it interest him so much?

'Well, be damned to that,' Henry said, 'so *that's* why she's here? But there's nothing in the Verney sale worth tuppence . . .'

'Now, Henry,' Annie said with a smile, 'I told you ages ago that the Hall was full of nice things.'

'Aye,' Henry said, 'so you did.' He looked at Matt. 'Let me know if you want me to pick you up this afternoon. 'Bye for now.'

He went out to his car. Nice things at the Hall. Nice enough to come all the way from Italy? It didn't seem likely.

Yet here she was, Francesca Zorelli from Rome. Signorina Zorelli, who said her business was buying things.

Chapter Four

The Verneys found the countryside around Beckindale very appealing. 'It almost makes you wish we could live here, doesn't it?' Charlotte said as they sat in their car on top of The Hallows and looked out over the moor.

'It's quite a view,' Gerald agreed.

'You know, darling, Guy is quite interested. There's no way, I suppose, you could keep the house and some land for him to try his hand at farming?'

'My dear girl, the Chancellor of the Exchequer has made that quite impossible. Guy will have to be content with inheriting my share of Precosolv. He can't be lord of the manor, I fear!'

'I suppose not. Seems a pity, doesn't it?'

He patted her shoulder. 'Don't get sentimental. Shall we go and take a look at the house? Last chance before the agents close it up for the public viewing of the auction.'

'Righto.'

The place looked mournful, with the furniture pushed hither and thither to make auctioneer's groups, carpets rolled up, and ornaments taken from mantel-shelves and cabinets to stand in rows on trestle tables.

'It's horrid,' she murmured. 'I wonder if ghosts of past Verneys are looking down on this?'

As if in response, a muffled sound from downstairs made them start. Then Gerald smiled. 'Not ghosts. That sounds all too human.' For whoever had come in was whistling to himself – Bach, it sounded like.

They went down to find a man in a clerical collar standing uncertainly by the doors of what had been the drawing-room. 'Ah, Mr Verney?' he said. 'I hoped to see you. I noticed your car going by a bit earlier.'

'You did?' Gerald said with amusement. 'How did you

know it was my car?'

'Oh, when you dropped by before – Mr Pearson saw you. He said, a dark red car. And no one else around here has a Jaguar.'

'My word,' Gerald said. 'Elementary, my dear Watson?'

The vicar chuckled. 'I suppose it sounds a bit over-inquisitive to you,' he said, 'but in a village like ours, we take an interest in our neighbours. I'm Donald Hinton, by the way.'

'Your parish?'

'That's right. How do you do, Mrs Verney?'

They shook hands. Hinton glanced about. 'How melancholy it looks, doesn't it? I didn't know it in its heyday, but Sam Pearson says it was a centre of local activity.'

'I suppose it was. I haven't been here much but Uncle George used to talk about things – I think he felt it was his duty to play his part.'

'But that's all over now.'

'I'm afraid so. Mr Rashley is dubious about getting the house off our hands – says no one wants a place this size these days. It looks as if it might stand empty for some time, which isn't good for the district, is it?'

'I see you understand the situation quite well, Mr Verney. There's a great deal of anxiety locally.' Hinton hesitated. 'I hope you're going to show some favour towards the tenants who want to buy their farms?'

Gerald and Charlotte exchanged a glance. Gerald couldn't help feeling a little guilty, and therefore aggrieved. 'I can't afford to do anybody any favours, vicar,' he said. 'I have to pay the death duties. The farms will sell for at least what they're valued at.'

'Oh, of course, I quite see that. I only meant . . . perhaps you'd see your way to letting them go at that and not having them bid up higher. Er . . . Mr Wilks tells me that if lots go for more than the probate value, that's an actual profit to you.'

'And who is Mr Wilks?' asked Gerald rather stiffly.

'Well, he's by way of being our fount of knowledge and general stand-by. He retired to the district six or seven years ago, I believe. Used to be in business and still keeps his hand in. Did he misinform me? About the probate?'

'No, as I understand it he's quite right. But it's a matter of swings and roundabouts, vicar. True, some lots may go for more than the stated valuation but others may go for less.'

'Not the agricultural land, surely. Land is not going to sell for less than its value, Mr Verney.'

'No . . . I suppose not.'

'It's just that the local people have seen strangers driving around looking at the farms. I daresay that if a syndicate came in to bid for the farms as an investment, they might go a lot higher than the tenants.'

'In an auction, Mr Hinton, the item goes to the highest bidder.'

'I . . . er . . . I thought the auctioneer could close the bidding at any point?'

'If I instruct him to, I suppose he could.'

'That is really what I was wondering, Mr Verney. If you could see your way to having the bidding closed when the tenant has made his bid?'

'Did they ask you to put this to me, vicar?'

'No, no,' Hinton said with a shocked glance. 'Not at all. It's just that I've listened to the chat in the village, and they're terribly worried about what may happen.'

'Well, I don't know whether I ought to discuss the thing with you at all, but I'll just tell you this, Mr Hinton. If the tenant can afford to offer for his farm at about or a little above valuation, I've no objection. But the fact is I've only heard of one tenant putting out any feelers. That's good agricultural land. I think they just don't have the money to buy at today's prices. They want to remain as tenants.'

Mr Hinton moved restlessly among the dusty furniture, his hands clasped behind his back. 'I see . . . Forgive me, I ought to mind my own business.'

'The welfare of your flock *is* your business – is that it?'

'Gerald,' Charlotte said in gentle admonition. 'Mr Hinton is naturally worried for his parishioners. But you see how it is, vicar. We're all in the same boat. We don't have the money to act as we'd like to – not any of us. I see that it's worrying for the tenants, of course. But the tenants are safe, aren't they, Gerald – they can't be ordered out or anything like that?'

'Good gracious, no. They've got decent leases, all of them. There's one that's thinking of buying, but even if he didn't his lease has eight years to go. Mind you, what renewals will cost them when the present leases expire, I don't like to think.'

Donald Hinton nodded and sighed. 'Well, well, we're letting ourselves be depressed by our surroundings. Let me invite you back with me to the vicarage for tea. Rather late in our relationship, I regret to say – tea at the vicarage just as your stay in the neighbourhood is drawing to a close.'

'That would be lovely,' Charlotte said before Gerald could refuse. She had rather taken to Mr Hinton. It must have required courage to walk into the Hall and beard its owner about the rights of the tenants. Even in this day and age, the lord of the manor wasn't to be dismissed as a nobody, but Hinton had put his points well.

Taken at face value, the Hall and all it stood for was a thing of the past. But the Verneys had influenced this part of Yorkshire for centuries and even now their actions could help or hinder. Charlotte knew that Gerald was very worried indeed over the money side of his inheritance. The amount due in capital transfer tax was frightening, and the dealings with tax officials and lawyers were time-consuming and tiring. She knew that he wanted to be finished with it all; perhaps he was being rather harder about the whole affair than he would have been in his own business dealings in London, simply because he felt overwhelmed here by responsibilities he'd never asked for.

She hoped that an hour's quiet chat with the vicar over tea would put things into perspective for him. She herself was a Londoner; she had no wish to remove to this part of the world and play Lady Bountiful. Yet she could feel the atmosphere of the house, was touched by the sense of something old and valuable crumbling away at last. It would be rather nice to leave Beckindale with goodwill all round, with the villagers understanding that the Verneys still wished them well.

They had tea in a delightful if shabby room that opened on to a garden with a lawn, roses, and a shrubbery. As Charlotte was standing by the window sipping tea, she saw an elderly man appear and begin delving about in the herbaceous border. 'I say,' she said, 'you've actually got a gardener?'

'What? Not at all?' The vicar joined her at the window.

'Oh, it's Mr Pearson. Sam! Sam! Come and meet Mr Verney and his wife.'

Sam, hearing the call, gave over his work. He was putting stakes in to protect the delphiniums, which were just about to come out. Always had good delphiniums, the vicarage garden. He took out his handkerchief, wiped his sweaty hands, and went to the French window.

'Come in, Sam. Like a cup of tea?'

'Now, that would be right grand,' Sam said. 'Mr Verney, Mrs Verney.' He shook hands. 'I knew your uncle well, Mr Verney. And his father afore him.'

'So I gather. You've seen a lot of changes, Mr Pearson.'

'Few of 'em for the better,' Sam sighed, stirring his tea.

'We can't know whether it's good or bad,' Gerald said. 'History will show.'

'Huh! History doesn't know much about how ordinary folks live. Kings and queens and battles, that's all that's in the history books. But folks' livelihood, and what's important to 'em – you don't get much on that.'

There was a prickliness in his manner that perplexed the vicar. From Sam's previous eagerness to show friendship to the Verneys, he'd have expected him to be more warm in his manner to them. He couldn't know, of course, that Sam's family were about to lock horns with the Verneys over a piece of land.

For his part, Sam was sizing up Gerald Verney. If there was going to be a fight, he wanted to know what the opposition was like. Henry Wilks had been to see the lawyer, Mr Jenkins, had put the problem to him, and they were now waiting to hear the ins and outs of it. Joe was furious about the whole affair. Sam had never seen his grandson so roused. Oh, aye, there'd be a right how-d'you-do over this, and it was as well to know whether Gerald Verney would be awkward.

Gerald wasn't aware of being inspected. But Charlotte was, and felt the same cool surveillance when later they went to the Woolpack for a drink before heading back to Connelton.

This time it was Henry Wilks who was sizing them up. He had some rather bad news to pass on to the Sugdens, so it wasn't a bad notion to be able to report on the character of their antagonist.

'What'll you have, dear? Gin and ton? Two gin and tonics, please.'

Amos fetched them. He had guessed at once who they were, and was wondering whether he could ask for an interview for the *Courier*. 'Can I get you anything else?' he asked.

'No thanks, that's fine.' Gerald paid. Amos made a little difficulty over counting out the change. Gerald said to Charlotte, 'Nice old place, isn't it? We've never been in here before on any of our visits.'

'That would be to t'Hall,' Amos said, leaping in.

'Quite right.' Gerald suppressed a smile. The vicar had said they took an interest. He hadn't been wrong.

'There's a lot of interest in the auction,' Amos said, nodding at one or two customers at tables on the far side of the saloon. 'Never had so many folk dropping in.'

'I must admit it surprises me,' Gerald said. 'There's nothing of any great value at the hall.'

'What, a great old place like that?' Amos protested. 'Must be full of antiques and obets dart.' He'd seen this phrase in the catalogue belonging to Mr Wilks, which he'd purloined for an hour's study. 'Objets d'art', it said. He'd no clear idea what that was, nor how you pronounced it.

'Oh, some Sèvres porcelain, I believe, and some quite good Hepplewhite.'

'Oh aye,' Amos said knowledgeably. Sèvres porcelain, that was cups and saucers, happen. But Hepplewhite? 'Dates back a bit, I reckon?'

'What, the Hepplewhite? Well, naturally. But there's not really much of it.'

'What we've got a lot of is ancestors,' Charlotte put in with a chuckle. 'Rows and rows of them, as Noel Coward said – but not Gainsboroughs and Lawrences, unfortunately. Really, Gerald, your family had the most unfortunate propensity to support local artists!'

'Or else do the painting themselves. Like Great-Uncle Oswald.'

'Really? You had a painter in the family? I didn't know that, darling.'

'If you can call him a painter. Those landscapes are by him.'

'Oh,' said Charlotte, and sipped her gin and tonic.

'Yes, oh. Talented amateur is the best you can say of him. From what I hear, he was a pain in the neck. Thought he was better than Rembrandt.'

'His paintings are in the sale?' Amos enquired, imagining a piece for the *Courier* – 'Beckindale's Victorian Past Preserved in Paintings by Talented Verney' – a bit long, that. Mr Towers was always asking for snappier headlines.

'Of course, "everything must go", as it says on the shop windows.'

'Oswald's offerings will go for about a fiver each,' Gerald said with a sigh. 'Worst of it is, there's a family legend that he destroyed some irreplaceable works of art.'

'Really? A mad artist, was he?'

'You can laugh, Charlotte, but Oswald's father or grandfather – which was it, now? Anyway, some predecessor . . . He'd been a collector of considerable merit. Family letters seem to show he brought back works of the Italian Renaissance from his European travels. Marbles, paintings . . . Not one of them left.'

'Gerald darling, that's awful! What happened?'

'Who knows? Oswald didn't like his ancestor's choice and either got rid of the things or destroyed them.'

'Destroyed them?' Charlotte certainly wasn't laughing now. 'You mean, took a knife to them? Put them on a bonfire?'

'Who knows? The story goes that he didn't approve of nudity. You have to remember that he was a Victorian, an enthusiastic churchgoer. It probably pained him to see statues of unclothed goddesses. Well, if you looked around on your visit to the Hall, I think you'd have to admit we Verneys were big on ancestors in uniforms and stodgy views of Riggindale. But not Venus unadorned.'

'What a shame, darling. No hope of finding them in the attics, I suppose?'

'The attics have been emptied, alas. Well . . . Going to have the other half?'

'If you are.'

'I'm driving, so I'll have a bitter lemon. Er . . . Amos . . . another gin and tonic and a bitter lemon.'

Amos didn't want to break off his conversation. It was

fascinating, all this background material about the Verneys. Whether it would make an article for the *Courier* was doubtful – Mr Towers preferred news about the present rather than nostalgia for the past. 'Mr Wilks,' Amos called, 'one gin and tonic and a bitter lemon.'

Gerald turned his head to watch Henry draw the spirits. 'So that's the famous Henry Wilks?' he remarked.

'Famous?'

'"Our fount of knowledge and general stand-by".'

'Eh?'

Henry, glad of the chance to join them, brought the drinks. 'Viewing begins tomorrow, then, Mr Verney,' he remarked.

'Yes, it does. Are you interested in buying anything, Mr Wilks?'

'Well, I'll go and have a look,' Henry said. 'Might be nice to have a memento or two here in the Woolpack.'

Amos cast him an affronted glance. If any purchases were to be made for the Woolpack, he expected to be consulted.

'What's happening about the sale of the land?' Henry asked, believing that direct frontal attack usually paid off.

'So far, very little,' said Gerald. Not another plea on behalf of the tenant farms, surely?

'Some of your property is scattered all over the dale, isn't it? Awkward for you when it comes to selling. I mean, a spread of a hundred acres is interesting, but little bits in plots of ten or twenty acres must be difficult to dispose of.'

'Oh, I suppose they might interest people who want to build houses,' Charlotte said, trying to help along the conversation.

'Not in Beckindale,' Henry said, shaking his head. 'They wouldn't get planning permission. This is an agricultural area.'

'Well, I leave all that to the agent,' Gerald said. 'No use keeping a dog and barking yourself. What I want is to get it cleared up and pay the tax. The sooner the better.'

'Ah,' said Henry. 'Yes, I daresay it's a burden hanging heavy on you.'

'You can say that again! There was an old fellow at the vicarage, was saying history books talk about battles and

55

kings but not about ordinary people. I think,' Gerald said with some bitterness, 'if someone wrote a book about how taxation has weighed on ordinary people, it might be very enlightening.'

'That would be Sam,' Henry ventured. 'He said he were going to the vicarage to tie up the delphiniums.'

'A Mr Pearson, I believe,' Charlotte supplied.

'Aye, that's him. He and his son wrote a very interesting book about the history of Beckindale.'

'Really? I must buy a copy,' said Charlotte.

'Oh, it's not out yet. Jack's still working on it. He's a perfectionist. Jack lives in Rome, you know. My daughter's there too. I . . . er . . . gather you lived there for a time, Mr Verney?'

'Oh, only intermittently. My father was a resident, though.'

'Yes. We have a lady staying at the inn – a Miss Zorelli – who says she has friends who used to visit the Hall. I mean, from Rome.'

'Zorelli? No, I don't know the name. Did she mention the friends' names?'

'No. She's out at the moment, or we could ask her.'

'It's true enough that Dad's friends used to stay with Uncle George from time to time,' Gerald agreed. 'It really is a small world, isn't it? Well, so long. Charlotte and I are expected for dinner at the Feathers.'

When there was a lull a little later Henry asked Amos if he'd mind being on his own for a while. 'I've some business to attend to up at Emmerdale.'

'If a busy time comes up, I'll try not to interrupt you,' Amos said in rather a huffy tone. 'I know you prefer not to be called upon when you're off on your own affairs.'

'Now, Amos, it isn't likely to get busy again until after nine.'

'With all these visitors in the area for the viewing tomorrow, I don't know how you can be sure of that.'

'Well, if you get inundated, ring me at Emmerdale and I'll be back in ten minutes.'

'Very well, Mr Wilks.'

The family at Emmerdale had been expecting his visit. They knew he had been back to see Mr Jenkins that afternoon, at the solicitor's request.

He found them collected in the farm kitchen. The evening meal was long since over but Annie had the kettle on for a cup of tea, and there were small cakes set out on a plate, almost as if it were a party instead of a council of war.

'I gather the news isn't good,' Joe said, 'or you'd just have passed it on to us by phone.'

'You're right, Joe. I had a very depressing session with Jenkins.'

'So what's the verdict?'

'Let the man have his cup of tea first,' Annie protested. She handed it to him, and he took it, leaning against the fireplace to drink.

'The long and short of it is, Jenkins sent a clerk to make a search of the deeds. And the deeds of the Verney Estate show that meadow as belonging to them.'

'That can't be right!' Joe cried.

'Here,' Henry said. He took from the pocket of his jacket a photocopy of a pen and ink map. 'That's a copy of the map filed with the deeds as required by law. Look for yourself. That field – in fact all the way from the Verney edge of the woods right down to the lane leading to the main road – is Verney land.'

'There you are,' muttered Sam. 'Verney's Land. I said so.'

'Listen, Henry,' Joe said, putting the map on the table, 'I can see that the paper shows the boundary on *our* side of the meadow. Yet t'fact remains that we've been farming that land for years.'

'Aye. We've been using twenty acres that don't belong to us.'

'Who'd have thought it possible?' Matt murmured.

'They do belong to us,' Sam protested.

'Not in writing, Sam.'

'Oh . . . that's just legal quibbles.'

'It's just unbelievable,' Joe muttered. 'How do we stand, actually?'

'We may have Right of Ownership. Jenkins mentioned a thing called Right of Adverse Possession.'

'And what does that mean when it's at home?'

'What I said before?' Matt suggested. 'Bit like squatting?'

'Not far off.'

'I'm not letting that word be used about our land,' Sam cried in a fury.

'Well, it's sort of like getting something by default. Verney hasn't stopped us from using the land – Jacob enclosed it all those years ago and farmed it. In a court of law, Jenkins says . . .'

'A court of law?' cried Annie. 'Don't say we have to go to court over it!'

'You're right, Annie. Nobody ever gains by that except the lawyers. It could cost a packet to defend our right to that meadow.'

'But we've got to have it, Henry,' Joe said in a calmer manner. 'It's part of the schedule of rotation of the farm. We get some of our best hay off that field, not to mention good barley. If we have to buy in what we get off that twenty acres, it could be a big blow to us.'

'There's no alternative to going to court over it, Henry?' Matt enquired.

'Well . . . that depends.'

'On what?'

'On how desperate Gerald Verney is.'

'What d'you mean?'

'According to Jenkins, who of course has got his ear to the ground concerning anything to do with Beckindale, Verney's London business isn't doing too well at present. Conditions are bad in the Mediterranean and the demand for cosmetic vegetable oils has gone down in any case. So I'd imagine the last thing Verney wants is to fritter away any of his inheritance on a court case.'

'What are you saying, Henry?' Annie asked. 'Say it straight out.'

'Well, I reckon Verney'd sell us the land at a reasonable price. Mind, I'm not sure of that, but I got the impression earlier this evening that he's anxious to be shot of it all.'

'Sell us our own land?' Joe groaned.

'But it may not be our own land. If he took us to court, he might win. Any road, it would cost us something to fight a court case so we may as well make him an offer to buy the land in the first place.'

'But it would cost him something to fight a court case too.

That would cut down his profit on the sale of the land,' Joe said, thinking out loud.

'You've got it, lad. Looking at it sensibly, it's in Verney's interest to let us have that meadow at a reasonable price. We can point out to him that if we go to court we'll probably win. That ought to make him see reason.'

'But the land appears on the Verney deeds as theirs,' Annie said. 'He might dig his toes in.'

'Well, if he does,' Henry said, and shook his head.

'How much could he sell it for if he could establish that it is still his?'

Henry put his empty tea cup down on the kitchen table with a thud.

'Twenty acres of prime farm land. How much an acre, Joe?'

Joe hesitated for only a moment. 'Thousand pounds an acre.'

'There you are then. He could sell it for twenty thousand pounds.'

The sum was too vast for them to take in. They all just sat there, looking at each other.

Chapter Five

Dolly had been out visiting an acquaintance in the village while the family conference was held. When she got back, it was fairly late so she and Matt went up to bed almost at once. Matt asked if she'd had a nice evening and showed an interest in what she told him – which was mainly about helping Maisie Briggs to choose wallpaper and paint for her redecorations.

But she could sense something wrong. As she sat brushing her hair by the dressing-table she could see Matt in the mirror, sitting on the side of the bed staring at his slippered feet.

'Well, love, are you going to tell me or aren't you?' she asked.

He turned his head, and in the mirror she met his eyes. They were deeply troubled. His round face was rather pale.

'Is it about Henry and the lawyer?' she enquired, for she knew of course that Henry had been dealing with the little mystery of the Top Twenty.

'Them posts,' Matt said.

'The ones we saw on the way back from looking at the Lodge? Listen, Matt, I were talking to Maisie about the Lodge, and she says she's been in it – when George Verney lived in t'Hall, the Lodge was in use and a Mr and Mrs Goodgrace lived there – looked after the grounds and did a bit of house-cleaning by way of rent, though of course they didn't have to open gates any more.'

'Aye,' Matt said, 'I think I recall them. White-haired old feller. Used to put prize-winning foliage into the Autumn Show, from t'shrubs in t'grounds.'

'Maisie says the inside were ever so nice! All on one floor, of course – be a bit like living in a bungalow, won't it?' She laughed with pleasure at the thought.

'Well . . . that's just it . . . Dolly, I don't think we're going to be able to afford it.'

'What?' She swung round on the dressing-stool to face him direct. 'But, Matt, even if we can't buy it outright, six thousand is a good deposit. We'd get a building society mortgage for the rest, surely?'

'It's not that, love. It's . . . well, I think we're going to need the money.'

'Need it? Who? Us? For what?' Her mind was wheeling. She was trying to work out what she and Matt could possibly need more than this little house to themselves. 'What d'you mean, Matt?'

'Henry's just been saying, Dolly . . . It's bad, about Top Twenty field. Grandad was right when he recalled it as being Verney's Land. T'lawyers looked at t'deeds. That land really does belong to Verney.'

'What?'

'Aye, Verney's Land. Seems we've been growing hay and cereals on it for quarter of a century, wi' no right to it.'

'But that's not possible, Matt!'

He shrugged, without replying to her protest. It was possible: they had done it.

Slowly she rose and came to sit beside him on the bed. 'What does it mean, Matt?'

'It means we're going to have to prove our right to it if we want to keep it.'

Dolly's quick wits had got to the nub of the matter almost by instinct. 'Emmerdale's been ploughing and sowing for twenty-five years, right? That establishes a title to the land, doesn't it?'

'The lawyers seem to think so, but if we had to prove it in court it could cost a packet.'

'How do you prove your title?'

'Well, Grandad hates the word, but we've been sort of "squatting" on the land for a long time. We've never paid any rent for it. So that makes it ours, I think. Verney hasn't bothered to claim it or re-claim it so the law would say he'd lost his right to it. I *think*.'

Dolly took his hand into hers and stroked it. 'Don't worry about it. It'll be all right. Henry's got a good head on him, and he'll work it out with the lawyers.'

'I dunno, love. He was just saying as Gerald Verney's a bit strapped for money. The man isn't going to let twenty acres of good land get away from him. I think he's going to make us pay for it some way. And Henry puts the price of a field like that at twenty thousand pounds.'

Convulsively her grip tightened on his hand. Now she knew why he thought their six thousand might be needed elsewhere. 'Oh, Matt,' she whispered.

'I'm not saying it's going to be that bad. But Henry's a bit worried, you can see that.'

'Could it . . . could Emmerdale manage without that field?'

'Oh aye. Manage. We could manage. But that's a very important bit of ground, Dolly. It'd make us a lot poorer, it'd cut down our income and spoil our farming routine if we lost Top Twenty. If worst comes to worst, we've got to pay Gerald Verney to keep that field.'

'Pay twenty thousand?' she gasped.

'We can't raise twenty thousand. I think Henry's hoping for some sort of a compromise. It's to do with the cost of going to law. If Mr Jenkins can convince Verney's lawyers that it's to his advantage to settle out of court because we have a good legal claim, we'll get the price down a lot, happen. But I think Joe's going to need that six thousand.'

Dolly made no reply.

'Will you mind a lot, love?' he asked.

It took her only a moment to find the right words. 'It'd be no use trying to settle down in a new house if your income had been cut so we couldn't afford the housekeeping,' she said with a little laugh. 'Nay, lad, I'd like to have the Lodge, but first things first, eh?'

He turned and took her in his arms. 'Ah, you're a lovely lass,' he murmured. 'The more I know you, the more I think I'm the luckiest man in the world.'

She let herself go into the joy of his kisses so as to blot out the disappointment she had felt. He might call her a lovely lass, but she knew how dismayed and resentful his news had made her. It was wrong of her – she ought to want to help the Sugdens if their farm was in danger. All the same, some selfish part of Dolly was murmuring, 'That's *our* money. Why should we have to give it up?'

She woke next morning in a hopeful frame of mind. Perhaps the lawyers would be able to scare Mr Verney into letting them keep Top Twenty. After all, more than twenty-five years of cultivation and never a penny's rent. That constituted a right to the field, surely. No arguing against that! Happen Verney would cut his losses rather than take it to court.

The conversation of the breakfast table turned on that, of course. 'I can't understand how all this wasn't noticed when Henry bought the farm freehold in the first place,' Joe declared, angrily sloshing marmalade on his toast.

'You can bet he's kicking himself now,' said Matt. 'But you know, he'd rely on his lawyers, and they probably didn't come and walk round the boundaries with him.'

'But they'd have maps like the one that shows Verney's claim.'

'Right enough. But then Henry wasn't familiar wi' the ground. He'd only been in the neighbourhood six months or so, if memory serves me right,' Sam pointed out.

'Oh, don't talk to me about your memory,' Joe groaned. 'You and Verney's Land!'

'Facts are facts, lad. What I'm saying is, Henry might well have had a good look at the map, but it wouldn't occur to him to say, "Have I seen you cutting barley on that top field because if so you've no right to." Henry was no farmer –

though he's learned a lot. I mean, if it's anyone's fault, it's ours. We should have gone into Hotten and registered our right to that field, if that's what you do.'

'Dad, would you like more bacon?' Annie put in.

'Nay, I've no appetite,' he said. He pushed his plate away. 'To think we should ever be in a row wi' the Verneys! I can't put my mind to it, somehow.'

'We're not in a row, Dad –'

'Depends how you look at it,' Joe said. 'One thing's for certain. I'm not giving up Top Twenty wi'out a fight.' He too pushed his plate aside and got up. 'I've got work to do.'

'You going to the View?' Matt asked.

'Oh aye! If I can find the time, I'll go and take a look at all the things that belong to Verney! Might as well, since he seems to own summat we thought was ours!'

Many another in Beckindale had had the same thought today – to take a look at the Verneys' possessions, to set foot inside the Hall, to be on the same level as the 'great folks' just for a few hours. When the agent unlocked the house at ten in the morning, there were already people hanging about awkwardly on the drive, and cars were parked in the area to the left which had once been the tennis courts. There were about a dozen strangers too, some of them men in business suits who might well be dealers from Leeds or Manchester. Although Gerald Verney kept averring there was nothing of value in the house, there were some pleasant things with possibilities for an antique dealer; these days lesser works were snapped up and re-sold at good prices. The catalogue mentioned Sèvres and Dresden, for instance; not rare or special pieces, but certainly worth a look. And Hepplewhite, too. Even if years of family use had scarred it a little, it might be worth a penny or two.

Francesca Zorelli was there, waiting to go in. Her flashing dark looks attracted many an eye, but she stood off by herself, the catalogue casually tucked under her arm.

She had proved a mystery and an irritation to Amos Brearley. True, when she came into the bar in the evening and settled down with a Campari, the other customers enjoyed her presence and her conversation. And equally true, she spent money: if she felt like a glass of champagne, she'd no objections to paying for the whole bottle though she didn't drink it all.

But she wouldn't explain herself. Amos had tried all his ploys on her, but she remained unnaturally reticent. Where did she vanish to in the daytime?

'Oh, I walk around, admiring the landscape,' she said when he tried to find out.

But she didn't wear shoes suitable for walking in the dales, and he knew for a fact she'd been spending a lot of time in Hotten Public Library reading in great old books of local history, because Nicky Oldsworth had seen her and told Amos.

'Local history?' Amos said. 'What on earth does she want wi' that?'

'How should I know?'

'Are you sure that's what she were looking at?'

'Certain. It were early closing and Miss Prior in t'Reference Room had to ask her to pack up and go. So she got up and went out and I passed the table where she'd been reading, and there it was – *Dwellings of the Dales* by some old rector of St Andrews in Hotten.'

It surprised Amos even more to discover that Miss Zorelli had been to the offices of the *Hotten Courier* to look at the bound volumes. Amos learned this when he took his weekly copy to the newsroom. The girl in charge of files always took his manuscript from him – it seemed to him the editor downright avoided meeting Amos to have a chat and sent this chit of a girl to collect his piece in the outer office. Sally said to him, 'That Italian girl you mentioned last week in your articles – '

'You didn't print it!' Amos broke in. 'Far too much is cut out of my piece – '

'That's nowt to do wi' me,' Sally said with a toss of her head. 'But she were here at the office.'

'Eh?'

'Her, Miss Zorelli. She wanted to see the bound volumes.'

'Of the *Courier*?'

'Aye. She's got some lovely clothes, hasn't she? Knit silk, that dress she were wearing. Must've cost a fortune.'

'What did she look at in the bound volumes?' Amos demanded, agog.

'How'm I supposed to know? She asked for the years 1830 to 1838 but we didn't have 'em all – there was a fire, tha knows. But she spent a while leafing through what we'd got. Dunno if it did her any good. She went away looking a bit dissatisfied.'

What could she be trying to find out? Was there some terrible skeleton in the Verney closet? Amos's imagination took wing. Could it be that that old Verney of the 1800s had married secretly in Italy when on his travels? Could there be an heir descended from that marriage, now seeking to establish a claim on the Verney estate? Henry had said Joe valued the agricultural land at more than a million pounds – that would be worth coming from Italy for!

This operatic plot gradually faded from Amos's mind on the bus back from Hotten as he recalled that Miss Zorelli had had friends who visited the Hall in the time of George Verney. Surely if there had been any claim of that kind, it would have been made before now, since the family was known in Rome. And then there was Gerald's father, who'd actually lived in Italy for years. Nobody'd ever gone up to him and said, 'Here, I'm your cousin and ought to have the Hall, not that George Verney living there now.'

Reluctantly Amos gave up his 'missing heir' theory. But there was *summat*! Nobody could ever convince Amos that a fashionable young lady like Francesca Zorelli had come to bury herself in Beckindale in the height of the summer just for the pleasure of the ham sandwiches Henry made.

Amos knew that Francesca was at the View because she'd admitted at breakfast she was going. 'Admitted' – well, at least she'd made no secret of it. But then what would have been the use, since Henry had said he was going, and Amos himself intended to turn up and get some details for a report to the *Courier*.

'Are you after any particular item, Miss Zorelli?' Amos had asked.

'Yes, some coffee, please,' she replied, deliberately misunderstanding.

He handed her a cup and put the coffee percolator in front of her. 'Want some toast?'

'No,' she said, with a restless little movement. 'I don't feel like eating, thank you, Mr Brearley.'

'You seem a bit edgy this morning?'

'I'm always edgy when I go to a sale.'

'Oh? Do much of that, then?'

'Oh yes. I told you, I'm in business to buy things.'

'And the thought of the sale at Verney's makes you nervy?' Henry put in, raising his eyebrows.

'An auction is always exciting.'

'But the sale doesn't actually begin for another three days.'

'Ah, well . . . We Italians, you know,' she said with a laugh, and buried her nose in her coffee cup.

When she had gone, Henry said to Amos, 'She's after something in the sale!'

'She's a dealer, like?'

'I had that thought myself, earlier on. But I've chatted a bit with her, and she seems to know nowt about china or furniture, and it's them that's the main items in the sale so far as I can gather.'

'What d'you think, then, Mr Wilks?'

'I've no idea, Amos. I'm just going to keep an eye on her at the View and see what interests her.'

When Henry got to the Hall, the prospective buyers had gone in and Francesca was in conversation with a tall, handsome middle-aged man by a group of jardinières in the conservatory. Henry strolled towards them casually. But all he heard was, 'I used to live around here at one time. Idle curiosity brought me in.'

'You have come from far away, then?' Francesca enquired.

'Not too far. I'm staying at Long Beck Cottage for the moment. Sort of a holiday.'

'I also, sort of a holiday. At the Woolpack.'

'Ah, yes. Amos Brearley still there?'

'Most decidedly so,' Francesca said with a smile and moved off.

For a moment Henry was tempted to stay with the stranger. It would be quite interesting to talk with someone who used to know Amos and had come back after an absence. But chiefly he wanted to know what Francesca was going to look at, so he stuck with her. He followed from room to room as she strolled through the house, and he'd be hanged if he could make out what she was up to.

As far as he could tell, she worked her way through all the rooms except the kitchen, and consulted the catalogue regularly. From time to time her path would cross Henry's. She never tried to avoid him.

'Not a bad engraving, that,' he remarked to her as they stood in front of a black and white study of Sheffield in 1780.

'Oh yes, it is quite good, if you wish to collect industrial history.'

'Is that your specialty?'

'No, I know little of engravings.'

'What is your field, then?'

'My field is whatever my client asks me to look at.'

'So you have a client?'

'What about you, 'Enry? Is there something here that interests you?'

He could have replied, 'It's you that interests me,' but he was addressed by the vicar at that moment and lost his chance.

The vicar had little interest in the items on display except a case of butterflies, which he felt he might buy if the price wasn't too high. The Rev. Mr Hinton's hobby was butterflies and moths. But he had something else on his mind as he moved beside Henry through the big house.

'Do you happen to know the Groves at all, Henry?' he asked.

'What, that young couple who've taken Gimbel's? I've seen 'em around. Why?'

'I'm just trying to get to know them. They don't attend church, unfortunately.'

Henry knew better than to press the vicar for information, but he could make one or two guesses. One of Mr Hinton's parishioners must have come to him with some problem or query concerning the Groves, and from what Henry had heard among the customers at the Woolpack, it could have something to do with Nicky Grove's roving eye. He seemed to be a bit of a lad with the girls, did Nicky Grove.

For instance, Nicky seemed to have tried his luck with Francesca. From something he'd heard from Amos, it seemed as if Nicky had actually followed her into Hotten one day.

Well, it was none of Henry's business. But it did seem a strange way for a busy young farmer to go on. Though, as a matter of fact, from what he gathered it was the wife, Winifred, who was the farmer.

Henry had to go back to the Woolpack. He was expecting a call from the solicitor around noon, to discuss the next step in the business of Top Twenty. Amos was hovering, although business was quite brisk in the bar.

'Well, Mr Wilks? Well?'

'Well what?'

'What did she look at? What's she after?'

'Nowt, as far as I could see, Amos. She walked round like the rest of us, examining one or two things.'

'You must have missed it, Mr Wilks. It takes the trained eye of a reporter.'

'Then you go and take a look! She's still there, or at least she was when I left.'

'You should never have left while she was still there, Mr Wilks!'

'Good lord, Amos, we're not keeping surveillance on her. She is a guest at the inn, after all. I'm beginning to feel quite guilty at suspecting her of anything, as a matter of fact. She's a perfect right to come to Beckindale and go to the Verney's sale and even buy something there, if she wants to.'

'But why be so secretive about it, then? Why go digging and delving about in the library and the *Courier*'s files and all that?'

'I don't know, but I can't see anything wrong in it.'

'Couldn't you . . . couldn't you ring your daughter in Rome and just . . . check up on her?'

To tell the truth, Henry was tempted. But he drew back. 'You'll have me as bad as you are, Amos,' he muttered, and went through to the back.

He was rather pleased when the man who had chatted with Francesca came in a little later with a very pretty lass on his arm. 'How do,' Henry said. 'Saw you up at the Hall, didn't I?'

'That's right. Sad, isn't it, to see any house like that. A shell . . .'

'Come on, now, Daddy,' the girl said. 'We didn't come to Beckindale to make you melancholy.'

'True enough. So what are you going to have, Pru?'

'Is the beer good here?' Pru enquired.

Henry could see Amos swell with indignation. 'It's a well-known brew,' he put in quickly, 'Monks.'

'Right, I'll have a half of that, then, thank you.'

'And so will I,' said her father.

The bar was busy for a while. Then Henry was called to the phone. It was, rather later than he'd hoped, Mr Jenkins.

'I've made some tentative overtures to the Verney solicitors,' Jenkins reported, 'and they're acting very surprised at our claim. In fact, their first reaction was to dismiss it as some kind of a try-on.'

'Good heavens!'

'Oh, I disabused them of that idea at once. They know, naturally, that I wouldn't link this firm with any hanky panky.'

'I should think not!'

'But they want a statement of our case. You see, we have nothing in writing, nothing at all. So I need what is known in the legal slang as "a legend". I need to know the history of this piece of ground. Please don't misunderstand me, Mr Wilks, but your statement would carry no weight. You've only been in the district a few years – am I right?'

'Yes, about six.'

'Who at Emmerdale knows the story?'

'Well, Joe can testify that they've been farming that field since he can remember. That's twenty-five years. But better yet, there's Joe Sugden's grandfather, Sam Pearson. He remembers when the land was incorporated into Emmerdale estate.'

'Can you bring those two to the office?'

'When?'

'The sooner the better.'

'This afternoon?'

'I'll see if I can fix it up. I'll ring you back.'

Sam was very unwilling to be involved. He regarded anything to do with the law as bound to lead to disaster. 'Nobody wins except the lawyers' was his maxim. But finally he was persuaded and the Emmerdale party set out for Hotten about three o'clock.

By that time Francesca Zorelli had come back to the

Woolpack, having driven to Connelton to have a decent lunch at the Feathers before returning to her lodging. Amos was busy tidying up so didn't try to corner her about her day's activities. He was turning over a few catch questions to ask her when the phone rang. He went to answer it. There were a few clunks and clinks and a voice said, 'Is that the Woolpack Inn, Beckindale?'

'It is, Amos Brearley proprietor speaking.'

'One moment please.' A pause, during which Amos thought he heard an official English voice speaking to someone else who replied in an Italian accent. 'You're through, caller,' said the English telephonist, 'your call to Beckindale is connected.'

'*Mille grazie. Allo?* Beckindale?'

'Aye, this is the Woolpack Inn,' Amos said with rising interest.

'May I speak to Miss Zorelli, please?'

He went to the foot of the stairs and called. 'Miss Zorelli! Call for you. From Italy, I think.'

She ran lightly downstairs and took up the receiver. Amos went back to his tidying up. But even if he'd wanted to he couldn't have stopped himself from eavesdropping, and he didn't want to.

At first Francesca spoke in excited Italian. Then the caller from Italy, who seemed, despite his grasp of Italian, to be either English or American, must have reverted to English, for Francesca said, 'Of course. I was there before the door was unlocked.'

So she was talking about the sale!

A pause while she listened. Then she said, 'Well, you can stop worrying. I'm almost sure I've found it.'

Found what? Found what? Amos was burning with curiosity.

But now she went back to Italian, and he didn't gather anything else. He hastily moved out of earshot before she put the phone back and crossed to the stairs. 'I go up now to have a little siesta,' she said. 'It has been a tiring morning.'

'Aye, walking round a big house is tiring,' Amos said, fishing.

'I quite agree.' And with that she went upstairs.

Amos swept vigorously and put away the broom. He was

70

going up to the View at the Hall. There was a mystery to be solved.

And who better than Amos Brearley, Special Correspondent of the *Hotten Courier*, to solve it?

Chapter Six

David Annersley and his daughter Pru had paused on their way home from their pre-lunch drink at the Woolpack. It was a fine English summer day, warm with a light breeze, the sky blue and flecked with small clouds, the fields shimmering and rippling in their yellowing gown of wheat and barley.

'It's beautiful,' Pru murmured. 'I quite see why you wanted to come back to it. In fact, I rather wonder you didn't bring us here for a holiday while Mother was alive.'

'Your mother didn't care for the English countryside,' David said. 'She liked a warmer climate, and I can't blame her, considering the trouble she had with bronchitis.'

'And how about you?' she enquired, taking his arm and walking him away from the car. 'Is it doing you good, being back in the old haunts?'

'Don't fuss about me, Pru. I only got a bit of a bump from – '

'From an absolute maniac who drove into you broadside on! It's a miracle you walked out of that wreck. When I saw it afterwards, I tell you – '

'Forget about it, my love. I've learned that you have to put things behind you and go ahead, not keep looking back. The next question is, are you enjoying it here? I hope you're not finding it dull.'

'Well, it's quiet. No one can deny that,' she said with a playful pout of her mouth. 'But then there's this great auction going to come off. That's going to be fun. I've never been to an auction before.'

'Don't expect it to be like Mentmore,' her father warned. 'From what we saw this morning, there are only a few things worth big sums.'

'I know, but even so – I'm looking forward to it. Shall you buy anything? Just for old times' sake?'

He shook his head. 'I've no great wish to own anything from Verney's.'

'But didn't you tell me you used to work on the estate?'

'My father did. I lent a hand from time to time, but not on a paid basis.'

Pru laughed aloud. 'It's so difficult for me to picture you doing odd jobs on someone else's property! I can just imagine what the men at Annersley's would think if they heard that!'

'I think they know already. I never made any secret of it, Pru. I made my money the hard way, because I knew all there was to know about agricultural machinery. You could say I learnt it by tinkering about with the old tractors on the Verney Estate. I expect I've mentioned that to the men in passing.'

'Is it nice, to come back as a rich man to the place where you were poor?'

He put his arm about her and gave her a hug. 'You're taking the mickey. Come on, let's get back to the cottage and you can unfreeze me some lunch.'

As they strolled back to the car, Nicky Grove was coming up the lane. His quick, handsome features creased into a smile at the sight of them. He always liked to smile at a pretty girl, and one who was about to step into an expensive Citroën was doubly attractive.

'Morning,' he said.

'Morning. Fine day.'

'Not bad. Soon be time to get the barley in.'

'Yes, I suppose so.' David cast a knowledgeable eye on the crop in the field next to the lane. 'Looks a bit thin, doesn't it?'

'Hasn't done too well,' Nicky agreed, his attention on Pru, whose slim hips in tight jeans were certainly an eyeful.

'This is Sugden's land, isn't it?'

'Nope, that's mine,' Nicky said, although it might have been more truthful to say it was his wife's. 'Sugden's is behind us and across the big road. Know 'em, do you?'

'I used to,' David murmured.

'Oh aye? Local man, are you?'

'I was born not far from here.'

'Brought the young lady to see where her family came

from? Like *Roots*, I mean.'

'Not quite. I didn't have to hunt around for my origins,' David said with a smile. 'How about you? Are you one of the local families?'

'No, moved in fairly recently – first year here. Grove's the name.' Nicky held out a hand, and looked expectant.

'Mine is Annersley,' David said, shaking. 'This is my daughter Pru.'

'Pleased to meet you.' He took care to get a chance to shake hands with Pru, who smiled a little at the extra pressure he put into it. 'You moving into the area?'

'No, we're just on holiday. Daddy's not been too well.'

'I see. Well, I hope you'll enjoy it. Perhaps you'd like to be shown around a bit some time, eh?'

Pru hesitated. Her father nodded imperceptibly. He didn't want to tie her down to acting nursemaid to him – it was only fair to let her meet some young folk.

'That would be nice,' she said.

'How about this evening?' Nicky said, believing you should always strike while the iron's hot. 'Sunset should be pretty good from up Grey Top.'

'Grey Top? Where's that?'

'It's just beyond the village,' her father said. 'The view is good from up there.'

He was telling her that he had no objections to her going. 'All right then,' she said, 'I'd love to come.'

'Drop by and collect you about eight, then? Where you staying?' He knew, in fact. Everyone knew there were visitors at Long Beck. He nodded as if he hadn't known it when she gave the address and helped her into the car when they made ready to drive on.

Not bad, he thought to himself, not bad. There's money there.

The interview at the lawyer's didn't go well for the Sugdens. Sam was a little scared at finding himself in a law office and got cross when asked to repeat his information several times over. 'What's the matter with 'em?' he muttered to Henry. 'They got cloth ears?'

'Hey-up, Sam. They've got to get it all down word for word.'

'You mean that young lady's taking down everything I say?'

'Of course.'

That only made it worse. Sure at first of his recollections, Sam began to get anxious. But one thing he was prepared to swear to: Sugdens had never paid any rent to Verneys for the Top Twenty field.

'See, it used to be like this,' he said. 'Tenants would turn up at the Hall on the morning of New Year's Day and Mr Verney would accept their rent for the coming year. He used to serve a special cake and that. Jacob and Annie would go every year.'

'Then how do you know the rent of the Top Twenty field wasn't added to the standing rent at some point?' Mr Jenkins enquired with sharpness.

'Because the amount of the rent never varied,' flashed Sam. 'They used to pay it in cash. It were tradition. Jacob'd go to the bank the day before, and draw out the right amount, and at the same time he'd buy a bottle of whisky to take to the Hall – like first-footing, tha knows.'

'You're sure the sum never varied?'

'I've told thee, haven't I?' Sam roared.

'Now, now, Mr Pearson,' soothed Jenkins, 'I have to be certain of my facts, that's all. So you would bear witness that the rent was never increased to allow for the land now called Top Twenty?'

'I'd swear to it on a stack of Bibles.'

'You have receipts?' Jenkins said, turning to Joe.

'Nay, my father wasn't much of a bookkeeper,' Joe said. 'If he kept receipts I never saw 'em. 'Sides, when Mr Wilks bought out the freehold and we went into a partnership, we threw away a lot of old paper from the dresser drawer.'

He heard the lawyer stifle a groan. 'Never mind,' Jenkins said, 'the Verney Estate must have kept books.'

'It's the Miffield Estate, actually,' Henry said. 'I bought the freehold from a larger company which includes the Verney Estate. It might actually prove a little difficult to get the information, because Miffield Estate was formed by the late Mr Verney – I mean the man I knew – simply to try to clear up the mess his father had made of the business side.'

'Well, well . . . We'll do the best we can,' said the solicitor, taking refuge behind his horn-rimmed glasses. But Joe got the impression he was decidedly depressed by the lack of verifiable information he'd been given.

After he'd taken his grandfather home he went out for a walk to get rid of his feelings of frustration. On his way he passed Top Twenty, and in a fit of furious resentment he marched into it and pulled up the first half dozen of the posts that had been hammered in. But they were buried deep, and after he'd worked himself up into a sweat struggling with the seventh it suddenly struck him what a futile endeavour it was. He kicked it with the toe of his boot, then turned away. No sense wasting energy on a childish demonstration like that. Whether the posts were there or not, Verney laid claim to the field.

He turned away from the Verney side of Emmerdale and went up over the slope to Holly Farm, where the Gimbels used to live. He espied Winn Grove shooing home a stray hen down a track along the field's edge.

'Hello, there,' he called. 'Got a traveller, have you?'

'She's a demon,' Winn said, pausing and straightening with a hand in the crick of her back. 'Every day I have to go out and get her. A fox will make off with her, and serves her right. It's not even as if she lays all that well!'

'Ma was saying she thought you needed to strengthen the feed for them. She used to tell Kathy that it's a bit cold for them this side of the dale. They need just a little extra to counteract the wind that catches your slope.'

'I never thought of that,' Winn said, frowning. 'My word, there's a lot to think of!'

'How're you doing?'

'We-ell,' she said. She was a pretty young woman, brown-haired and clear-skinned, but her prettiness was marred by a habitual expression of anxiety. She, too, wore jeans, but unlike Pru hers were not fashionable – they were stained and shapeless, worn as the most suitable attire for her daily work.

'What do you think of our barley?' she asked, leading Joe to the crop growing against the track.

He picked a head and rubbed it between his thumb and fingers. 'Not bad. I reckon there's twenty grains a head there.'

'I was hoping for twenty-five.'

'Aye.'

'How many grains is yours?'

'Twenty-five, twenty-six.'

She sighed.

'You can't get farming right overnight, Winn,' Joe said to comfort her. 'It takes time.'

'I just feel we haven't got so much time, though.'

'Happen Nicky ploughed a bit too deep here.'

'Tell him that, Joe.'

'I did, as a matter of fact,' he replied, thinking how unimpressed Nicky had been at the information.

'And what did he say?'

'It were sown by then,' Joe said with a shrug, 'so nowt he could do, was there?'

'I'm wondering if I'll have enough feed for the winter. I don't fancy having to buy any.'

'I know what you mean,' he sympathized. 'Prices are scary, aren't they? But happen we can help you out if you get stuck. That is,' he added in an afterthought, 'if we aren't in trouble ourselves.'

She took that to be a joke. 'Not likely, is it? Oh, I wish I could get things right first time! I can't afford to make many mistakes.'

'None of us can,' he said with a sigh. 'Trouble is, mistakes have a way of coming up at you from nowhere . . .'

'You starting to harvest?'

'Two weeks' time, I think. The combine's coming on the Wednesday. Are you booked for it?'

'I asked them to come directly after you.'

'Who's going to drive it? Nicky?'

'Nay, we'll pay the firm. He's not had your experience, nor Matt's.'

Joe nodded.

'Joe . . .'

'What?'

'You know this sale at Verney's?'

'Yes?'

'Miffield Estate is the same thing, isn't it?'

'That's right.'

'We had a letter from Miffield Estate the other day, asking if they could send a man to look around.'

Joe frowned. 'Say what for?'

'No. But . . . I were thinking . . . with the sale and everything . . . do you think they want to do anything about altering the lease?'

'Such as what? They can't do owt. A lease is a lease. What have you got – five years?'

'Yes.'

'Then you've nowt to worry about.'

'But if they see the farm isn't doing too well, Joe – '

'That's nowt to do with them as long as you keep paying your rent on time. You haven't fallen behind in that, have you?'

'No, not so far. It's just . . . I don't know why they should send anyone.'

'Don't let it worry you,' Joe advised. 'You're okay so long as your lease is in order, and as you just recently signed it there can't be any problem.'

After he'd left her it struck him as ironic. There he was, telling her she'd nothing to worry about, when he himself was in all kinds of trouble with the Miffield Estate.

Nicky Grove strolled home as Joe was leaving. 'What did he want?' he enquired.

'Nothing, he was just out for a walk.' She went indoors with him and began preparing tea. 'I asked him about that letter from Miffield Estate,' she went on.

'I don't know why you're getting in such an old umpty about that. It just says they're sending a feller to discuss the tenancy.'

'Oh, you don't seem to see!' she broke out. 'Things are changing around here. Everything in that big house is being sold up, and you can bet there are all sorts of folk looking at the land and wondering whether to buy.'

'Well, they can't buy our farm, and that's a fact. You've got a lease, haven't you?'

'Yes, you know I have, but – '

'A bit late now, isn't it?' he said with resentment. 'All of a sudden you want my opinion. But you didn't pay much heed when you decided to go ahead and pay out for the lease.'

'Nicky, it was time to start out on our own. And this is a good little farm. We can make a good living here if you'll just – '

'If I'll just what? Slave twenty-four hours a day? You know as well as I do that I wasn't the one who wanted to strike out on our own. Happy enough to draw a weekly wage, me. But not you, oh no.'

'But we weren't getting anywhere, Nicky!' She ran a hand through her already tousled hair. 'We'd have been the same twenty years from now – going out to work and having almost nothing to show for it.'

'What have we got now? Two hundred acres on lease, that's been let run down –'

'But we can make a good thing of it.'

'And another thing! Why can't you for goodness' sake tidy yourself up a bit? Do you have to go round looking like Orphan Annie?'

She looked down at herself. 'But there's not much point wearing good clothes for milking or mucking out.'

'But you're not doing that now, are you? You've finished milking. Why can't you tidy yourself up and look . . . well . . . a bit like a woman?'

She was about to flare at him that if he'd been there to help with milking she could have been finished earlier, and perhaps had a bath and done her hair. But she checked herself, because they'd had this argument or one very much like it a hundred times before, and she knew it got them nowhere. She was having to face the fact: Nicky just didn't want to make a go of the farm. It would please him if they went broke and had to move out. It would even please him if this man coming from the Miffield Estate made some demand for extra rent so that they couldn't afford to go on.

Joe Sugden hadn't had to hurry back to Emmerdale because milking today was in the capable hands of Matt and his mother. He strolled on by the footpaths and came at last to the farm in time for tea, to find the family conferring with Henry. Joe said little in the discussion. He was too fed up. Then it struck him that Dolly was rather quiet. Probably she was bored to death with this continual nattering about Top Twenty so, to change the subject, he said to her: 'Been able to get the key so as to have a look inside the Lodge yet?'

To his surprise, instead of turning to him with animation, Dolly simply shook her head. 'Matt and I decided to leave

78

that for the moment,' she said.

'Oh?' Joe was puzzled, then saw what he thought was the explanation. 'Oh aye, I see – a bit difficult to be trying to buy a house from him on the one hand and arguing with him over ownership of a piece of land on t'other.'

That had, in fact, never occurred to Dolly. All she knew was that the money wasn't likely to be available. Now it struck her that even if the matter was settled without using Matt's savings, contacts with the Miffield Estate weren't likely to be very cordial. They wouldn't put themselves out to make it easy for Matt to buy the Lodge.

To cheer everyone up, Joe suggested they should go down to the Woolpack for a drink after tea. Matt and Dolly took it up, and Henry of course had to get back to help Amos.

The intention to spread good cheer was a bit dashed on finding Gerald Verney already there with Mrs Verney. He raised his glass to them as they came in, and Joe forced himself to nod in reply. But he couldn't help feeling a coolness towards this man, who already had so much and now seemed to want to take a piece of land from them that he'd never even seen.

'Mr Wilks!' Amos greeted Henry with some indignation. 'When you said you were going to talk to t'lawyer in Hotten, I didn't think you'd be gone all this time!'

'I'm sorry, Amos, I had to go to Emmerdale afterwards to talk over the results.'

'It was about Emmerdale, then?' Amos said, surprised. So far not a word had been breathed to him about the argument over Top Twenty field. Henry didn't want it noised abroad – and one way of having it known as if the town crier were calling it out was to let a word slip to Amos.

'Well, we've got a bit of a problem,' Henry confessed. It was as well to prepare the ground. Because if things went badly and they had to go to court, Amos would have to know.

'Problem? What sort of a problem?'

'This selling up of the Hall and the Verney property is having an effect on Emmerdale. I can't say more, Amos, because the lawyers have got to get together over it, but the sale –'

'Aye, and speaking of that,' Amos broke in at once. He

was dying for a chance to tell Henry about Miss Zorelli's phone call. 'There's something I've got to tell you.'

'About the sale of Verney's land?'

'Nay, about the auction! And why Miss Zorelli's here.'

Henry was quite taken aback. His whole mind had been so taken up with the meeting at the solicitor's office that he'd really forgotten about Miss Zorelli. 'What about her?' he said.

They were interrupted for a moment by an influx of customers, among them Pru Annersley, who bought herself a half of bitter and found a seat not far from Joe, Matt and Dolly. Joe cheered up. A pretty girl, new to the district, made something to think about other than the Emmerdale land.

When everyone had been served, Henry turned back to Amos. 'What was that about Francesca?'

'I know why she's here, Mr Wilks.'

'You do?'

'Aye, she's after summat in the auction!'

'Well, we guessed that.'

'She had a phone call this afternoon,' Amos reported, 'from Italy. Talked a blue streak in Italian for a bit and then said, clear as anything, "I think I've found it." '

'Found what?'

'Dunno. She didn't say. But I went up to the Hall afterwards to have a look round at what's on sale, and you know, Mr Wilks, there's nothing there looks up to much.'

'The porcelain,' Henry suggested. 'And some Hepplewhite chairs.'

'She said "it", not "them". And I had a word or two with some of the dealers from Manchester – in my capacity as correspondent of the *Courier*, you know – '

'Oh, of course,' Henry agreed.

'And they said the Hepplewhite chairs would fetch a bit, and that china you mentioned, and happen a bit for some of the bric-a-brac. But they didn't seem to think there was owt there to get excited about.'

'Hardly likely to tell you about it if there was, were they? It'd queer their pitch.'

'That's *it*, Mr Wilks,' Amos cried in triumph. 'Don't you see, that's the very point. That explains why Miss Zorelli's been so secretive. There's summat at t'Hall that's valuable, and she's the only one as knows.'

'What?' Henry said, struck by the unexpected logic from Amos. 'What makes you say she knows?'

'What she said. She said "I've found it." Not, "I've seen it" or "I've taken a look at it." It's not one of them items in the catalogue where they've praised it up so as to attract experts who'll want to bid up for it. It's summat nobody knows about – except her.'

'But how could she know?'

'Well, I haven't worked that out yet, but she's been doing a lot of reading up on Beckindale, hasn't she?'

'But what could it be? I've been up and had a look, and though I'm no expert I think I know antiques when I see 'em, and most of the furniture at the Hall is Victorian – good of its kind, but not exceptional.'

'All I can tell you is that she said, "I've found it," and right pleased with herself she sounded. But then she went into Italian again and I didn't get the rest.'

'You didn't get – ! Amos, were you eavesdropping?'

Amos looked affronted. 'Nowt o't'sort! I just happened to be sweeping up in the bar . . .'

'And you took care to sweep as near as possible to the phone.'

'If her voice is a carrying voice, can I help it, Mr Wilks?'

Henry shrugged, and went to fetch himself a Scotch. What Amos said was interesting, but so what? The item would show up in the sale and the dealers would catch on when it was displayed.

'What I want to know, Mr Wilks,' Amos said, pursuing him along the counter, 'is whether I should tell Mr Verney?' He nodded to where Gerald and Charlotte were sitting.

'You can't do that,' Henry protested. 'You eavesdropped on that girl's private conversation. You can't go bandying it about.'

'But if there's summat of value at the Hall and he doesn't know it?'

'Listen, Amos, that girl is a guest in our house and an acquaintance of my daughter's. If we're going to go round spying on her, it's a bit much.'

'Spying?' gasped Amos.

'I'd advise you to forget what you heard. It's the

gentlemanly thing to do.'

Amos very much wanted to do the gentlemanly thing, of course, but he also wanted to be a part of some great drama involving the Verneys. He was called away to serve some visitors, and Henry took his whisky to socialize with Mr Verney. It seemed to him that the better they could understand each other, the better the chance of an amicable settlement of the Top Twenty matter.

Gerald looked up as he approached. He smiled, his expression rather ironic. 'Sit down, Mr Wilks. I rather wondered if you'd make an opportunity for a word.'

'Oh?' said Henry, obeying.

'The solicitor that manages Miffield Estates got in touch with me late this afternoon at Connelton. There seems to be some notion that you're collecting material for an objection over the sale of that meadow up by Verney Wood.'

'We hope to prevent the sale,' Henry admitted. 'That land belongs to Emmerdale Farm.'

'It certainly does not, Mr Wilks. I'm afraid you're mistaken.'

'Look, I know the deeds of the Verney property show it as incorporated in the Verney Estate, but – '

'Yes, I hear you had a search made at the land register. If you had come to me in the first place, Mr Wilks, I could have saved you all that trouble.'

'But we had to have the right information, Mr Verney. All of a sudden we find workmen driving posts into the field, which we've farmed for more than a quarter of a century – '

'Quite right. But I could have put you right. After all, I *am* a businessman. I went through all the papers when I first inherited. And I can assure you that that field belongs to the Verney family.'

'I think you're wrong, Verney,' Henry said, getting a little hot under the collar. The man was so sure of himself! It was infuriating. 'I think we could establish our right to that field, since we've had the use of it for so long without paying rent. It's called Right of Adverse Possession.'

'I know what it's called,' Gerald said, growing a little heated himself. It was really too bad. Here he came into the district, forced to sell up because of this ghastly burden of taxation, and the local people were grabbing at what they could get.

'Darling, people are looking,' Charlotte said, laying a pacifying hand on his.

Gerald glanced about. True enough, some of Amos's customers were turning their heads to see what the loud voices were about.

Gerald took a hold of himself. 'My solicitor has explained what he believes to be the basis of your claim,' he said in a calmer manner, 'but I'm afraid you're under a misapprehension. That can only apply when no rent has been paid. And Emmerdale Farm has been paying the Verneys for the use of that land ever since it was first taken over by them.'

'You're wrong there!'

'I hardly think so. The Sugdens were tenants of the Verneys for generations.'

'But no extra rent was asked for or paid when Top Twenty was included in the farm. Mr Pearson is sure of that, and the account books must surely show it.'

'A tenancy is still a tenancy, Wilks, even if it's only a peppercorn rent for a single field.'

'Peppercorn?' Henry repeated, a faint chill striking him.

'I haven't got the letter with me at the moment. When I first inherited I took a lot of the documents home with me to London. But I can produce it.'

'Look here, there's a mistake. What sort of peppercorn?'

'A bottle of whisky. Every year when the rent was brought to the Hall, Mr Sugden brought a bottle of Scotch as extra payment for that meadow.'

Henry was stricken to silence. It had just that sound to it that might be truth – the casual, easygoing arrangement of old-world squire and tenant relationships.

'When the freehold was bought by you and the main farm property became Emmerdale Farm Limited, the whisky was still brought to the Hall on New Year's Day. I can't say who brought it. All I know is that my uncle once offered me a drink from a bottle that he said had been handed in that morning by the Sugdens.'

'I can't believe it.'

'I think you'll have to. I imagine when my uncle went to the South of France, the practice died out. But that's only a couple of years ago – not nearly long enough for you to establish a rent-free occupation of the meadow.'

'By heck,' Henry said.

'Now, you'll understand, I can't let that kind of agreement continue,' Gerald said crisply. 'We're both businessmen. You'll not dispute that a rent like that is unrealistic in this day and age. Considering the cost of farmland.'

Henry sat, wordless.

'So either you'll have to pay a proper rent for the land, Mr Wilks, or you can buy it. And you'd better make up your mind quickly, because if I get a good offer for that piece in the meanwhile I shall take it.'

Henry picked up his glass, swallowed the remainder of his whisky, then looked at Gerald. 'Aye,' he said. 'I'll think on.'

He rose and went behind the bar. There he began to get himself a refill.

'Mr Wilks!' protested Amos. 'You've had one already!'

'And this is the second. I'll pay, Amos. Don't let it worry you.'

'Did Mr Verney say summat to upset you?'

'Well, he certainly didn't make my day for me,' sighed Henry.

And not another word could Amos get out of him.

Pricked on by his own desire to have a conversation with Mr Verney of the Hall, Amos made it his business to collect the dirty glasses first from the table where Joe and Matt and the others were sitting. At the next table Gerald and Charlotte were having a slight argument.

'I thought you were a bit high-handed, darling,' she said.

'Good heavens, it *is* my land, Charlotte! The way he was trying to put it, I was going to be done out of it.'

'Oh, of course, you established your rights, I'm not objecting to that. But did you have to face him with an ultimatum?'

Amos leaned across to gather up glasses. 'Er . . . Mr Verney . . .' he began.

'What is it?' Gerald said, and then, in irritation, 'Oh, we've not finished with these.'

'Oh . . . er . . . it's not your glasses . . . It's . . . Mr Verney . . . About the auction . . .'

'What about it?'

'I were at the View this afternoon, and there's nothing to

the naked eye that seems very important.'

'I'm sorry you think so,' Gerald said more sharply than he intended. 'Let's hope the dealers who've been gathering don't share your view.'

'It's about them – the dealers – you see, I happen to know –'

'I'm sure your knowledge of antiques is extensive,' Gerald said. 'If you bid along with the others, you'll have an equal chance.'

'Oh, I'm not asking to get in ahead of anybody,' Amos said, catching on to what Gerald was thinking. 'No, it's only that I have reason to believe –'

'Excuse us,' Gerald said, getting up, 'it's getting late and we haven't eaten yet. Come along, Charlotte, let's get back to Connelton.'

With a frigid nod, Gerald led the way out. Amos stood with the tray of glasses. After a moment he gathered up the two that Gerald and Charlotte had left.

Very well, if he didn't want to be told that he had a hidden treasure somewhere, too bad for him!

Chapter Seven

Joe was a bit disappointed to find that Pru had a date for later that evening, and more than a little alarmed when he learned that it was with Nicky Gove. She hadn't struck him as the sort of girl who would take up with a married man, but there you are – in these days, it didn't seem to matter.

When Henry took him aside and told him what he'd heard from Gerald Verney, Joe's gloom was complete. 'What happens now?' he asked.

'Well, he'll have to produce the evidence. He says it's in London. I reckon he'll ring home – or happen he's done that already – and ask to have it sent on to him. Tomorrow or next day, we should get a look at it. If it exists.'

'Oh, it exists all right,' Joe said. 'At least, it's certainly a fact that us Sugdens have taken a bottle of whisky to the Hall every year. I even remember being sent wi' it when Dad were took bad. I handed it in to the housekeeper. The Verney Bottle, it were called.'

'Joe . . . Why didn't you tell me?'

'How was I to know?' Joe groaned. 'I thought it were just some old tradition. I didn't know it were thought of as rent.'

There was nothing more to be said for the present. Joe took his leave and drove himself to Hotten to see a film – not that he enjoyed it. When he got home to Demdyke Row he was tired and disheartened. What was the use of anything? You worked and worked, but all you got was hard knocks.

The viewing days at the Hall came to an end, the sale proper began. Everyone in the district tried to drop in on it for at least some part of their time, because it was quite a thrill.

Joe was staggered at the prices. 'Thirty-two thousand pounds for eight chairs?' he marvelled aloud to Matt as they walked down the drive after the dining-room furniture had come under the hammer.

'Aye, I thought I was rich with six thousand pounds in the bank.'

'You know who nearly got 'em?' Joe said. 'That Italian lady Amos is always wondering about.'

'Did she? I didn't hear her pipe up?'

'Oh, they seldom say owt. Nods and winks, that's all. But she went up to thirty thousand before she dropped out.'

'Is that why she's come, then? To buy stuff at the auction?'

'I suppose so. I wonder if that price was what the probate valuer thought?'

'I reckon they know more or less the value of stuff like that, don't they? So if I understand Henry rightly, that means Gerald Verney won't make much on it. Tax will run off with most of it.'

Joe nodded. He didn't want to discuss Gerald Verney. Tomorrow that gentleman was to come to the farm with the letter which proved he was the owner of the Top Twenty meadow. It stuck in Joe's throat that this piece of land was probably going to bring in an unexpected profit to Verney. If the government valuer had accepted that the peppercorn rent could not be set aside, then Top Twenty had been assessed as having almost no value to the Verney Estate. Now, if the Sugdens were going to have to pay a proper price, that was pure profit to Verney, because anything in excess of the probate was not subject to capital transfer tax.

Amos had come to the auction today because Francesca

was here this morning. But he'd been perplexed when she bid for something that was on the catalogue as an acknowledged target – a group of eight Hepplewhite chairs. Amos was astounded at the price they fetched, but all the same his main interest was in what secret treasure she was after.

But the sale went on and she didn't bid again. She moved away to wander through the house, where the succeeding lots were still standing with their labels and tags showing catalogue numbers.

Amos, all his journalistic instincts roused, followed her at a distance. Francesca was either unaware of him or didn't think he mattered. She paused at last in front of a row of paintings standing against the wall. She stooped, and stared attentively at one of them.

Amos sauntered up and began studying the paintings at the other end of the row. They were a group of six landscapes, insipid and only adequate in execution. All were local scenes. Amos even recognized some of them, although houses had changed or been built since the painting was done. He flipped through his catalogue.

'No. 901. A landscape by Mr Oswald Verney, "Moorland View". Dated 1893.'

Francesca looked up as if seeing Amos for the first time. 'Ah, Mr Brearley. You are interested in art?'

'Oh, very,' lied Amos. 'These are very good, aren't they?'

'Do you think so? I should have thought they were extremely amateurish.'

Amos moved along the row to take a look at the painting she'd been examining. 'No. 904. A landscape by Mr Oswald Verney, "Dillingham Crags". Dated 1894.'

'Er . . . Mr Oswald Verney – he was an ancestor of Mr Gerald,' Amos said. 'Makes it interesting, does that.' He looked at her hopefully.

'Does it? Perhaps it does.'

'It's a very pretty picture, don't you think?'

She gave him a brief, enigmatic smile, scarcely more than a curving of her full lips. 'But beauty, Mr Brearley, is only skin deep.'

With that she walked away. Amos was left scratching his head in perplexity.

He had to go back to the Woolpack to get ready for

opening. Henry was just hanging up the telephone receiver as he came in. He looked a bit grim, to Amos's way of thinking. But he was too full of his own news to pay much heed.

'Listen, Mr Wilks, I think I've found out what it is that Miss Zorelli wants to buy in the sale.'

'Oh, not again, Amos . . .'

'But I saw her looking at it! I did, Mr Wilks!'

'What, then?' Henry asked, despite himself.

'It's them paintings by Mr Verney.'

'Who?'

'Oswald Verney. He were great-uncle to Mr George. Quite a talented amateur, I should say.'

'Should you, Amos?' Henry replied. 'I had a look at those, and thought they were nice enough but no great shakes.'

'But I tell you she were leaning down looking at them. At least, one of 'em – "Dillingham Crags", painted in 1894.'

Henry took the glass cloths off the pumps. 'Well, if she's come all the way from Rome to buy that, we'd better stand back and let her have it. Don't knock her over in the rush, I mean.'

'You think there'll be a lot of bidders?'

'There'll be one, according to you – Francesca. Other than that, I can't imagine anyone wanting it, except happen the local museum because it's of historical interest.'

Amos was flummoxed. 'But it must be that, Mr Wilks. She were looking at it right intent.' He paused, deep in thought. 'Happen there's something painted into it – a map, like, or a code.'

'You what?' Henry said, giving up his activities to turn and gape at Amos.

'Well, it must be *something*! I know! It'll be them art treasures that Oswald did away with! Happen there was one of 'em he didn't get rid of. Hadn't the heart, mebbe. So he put it somewhere safe and painted the whereabouts into that landscape. That's it, that's it – it's buried on Dillingham Crags!'

Henry went to him and put a hand on his shoulder. 'Get a grip on yourself, Amos,' he said, quite kindly. 'There's nothing less likely than that Oswald Verney buried anything on Dillingham Crags. For one thing, he was a fat old boy who never went out if he could avoid it, by all accounts. For another, why should he bury it there when he had all the house and grounds to hide it? And lastly, why should he want to? Tell me that.'

'Well . . . er . . . there could be a purpose.'

'Give me one.'

Amos couldn't think of a single one. He said lamely, 'Well, there must be some other reason. But she were interested in that painting, that I do know.'

'As far as I'm concerned,' Henry said, 'if she's found a hidden treasure among the belongings of Gerald Verney, she's welcome to it. But she'll be lucky if she gets it, because it seems to me Verneys hang on to what's theirs.'

'Summat wrong, Mr Wilks?' Amos asked, sensing at last that Henry was depressed.

'Oh, nothing much. Just that Gerald Verney now has the document here that proves he's been paid rent for a bit of Emmerdale.'

Amos nodded and went into the kitchen to put on the kettle for a cup of tea. Then he reappeared, kettle in hand. 'That can't be right,' he objected. 'You and the Sugdens own the freehold of Emmerdale.'

'Not all of it, it seems.'

'What d'you mean?'

'The field next to Verney Wood seems to belong to Verney. It's been rented from him all this time without anyone being aware of it.'

Amos shook his head. 'Rent's rent. You can't pay it without knowing it.'

'You can if it's a bottle of whisky that you've handed over every year.'

'Whisky?'

'It seems Jacob Sugden made some sort of agreement with old Mr Verney to pay him a bottle of whisky every year for the right to use Top Twenty field.'

'Ah,' Amos said, and went to fill his kettle. When he had put it on the stove he came back into the bar. 'I wonder where Jacob bought the whisky?' he said. 'He didn't get it here!'

Annie Sugden had looked in at the auction that morning. She had no intention of bidding but wanted to see what it was like when a great house was sold off to the highest bidders. On her way home she dropped in at the Woolpack as it opened for midday business.

'I tried to ring you,' Henry said. 'There was no reply.'

'No, Matt and Joe went to the auction and then on to Hotten. Dolly was to meet Matt there. As to Dad, you know what he's like – he often doesn't hear the phone so as not to have to answer it!'

'What'll you have?' Amos enquired.

'Sherry, please, Amos. Did I see you at the auction?'

'Aye, but I didn't stop long. I was scared they thought I was bidding for summat. Seemed to me, if you so much as scratched your nose, you'd end up wi' a set of Victorian fire-irons.'

'I wanted to get you,' Henry resumed, 'to tell you Verney's been in touch. He's got that letter.'

'I see.' She said it quite calmly. She'd long ago come to terms with the idea that Gerald Verney could establish his right to the Top Twenty meadow and would have to be paid in some way. That didn't mean she enjoyed the prospect. She could tell it was going to be a costly business. 'What happens next?'

'He wants to present the "evidence". I asked him to call at the farm this afternoon. Is that all right?'

'Yes, of course. It'd be best if we were all there and heard the rights and wrongs of it at one go.'

'That's what I thought.'

'What do you think will happen?'

'Well, he'll want something out of it. Something substantial. But on the other hand, that field isn't really any good to anyone except us. I mean, one isolated field isn't much of an attraction.'

'Except for grazing.'

'But nobody's going to pay him much to rent grazing rights, Annie.'

She looked doubtful and sipped her sherry. Amos, having attended to a refill for Old Walter at the far end of the bar, came to join her. 'I was with that Miss Zorelli at the auction,' he said. 'Is she still there?'

'No, they've broken off for lunch. She drove off towards Hotten in that little Fiat of hers.'

'It's the painting she's interested in,' Amos began.

'Now, Amos, don't start all that again,' Henry warned. 'Shall I start on the lunch?'

'Aye, might as well. I did the potatoes earlier. If you don't mind, Mr Wilks, keep an eye of 'em this time and don't let them go to soup.'

'I'll do my best. I'll see you later on, then, Annie?'

'Aye – what time?'

'I think it'll be about half-three.'

Henry went to the kitchen while Annie finished her sherry alone. She refused Amos's offer of another and went to the door. Just as she reached it, it opened and someone came in.

Annie drew back. She felt as if a wave of shockingly cold water had gone over her. Her hand went up to her throat. Then, half-recovering, she moved on and went out.

The man who had come in had been just as keenly affected. He stood stock still after she had gone, then came rather slowly to the bar.

'Morning,' Amos said, looking at him with avid interest. What could it all mean? Annie had been knocked all of a heap at sight of the newcomer. 'What are you having?'

'Half of ale, please.'

'Liked it, did you? Your daughter were in the other night for another sample.'

'Yes, she told me.' He paid and took a drink.

'Don't I know you?' Amos said. 'I thought before, when you came in, as you were someone I ought to know.'

'You wouldn't remember me. You were new at the Woolpack then, and I left almost immediately after. Annersley's the name.'

'Oh aye? Farmed around here?'

'No, I was in one of the cottages on Verney's estate. My father worked for him.'

'You knew the folks hereabouts, though?'

'Oh yes.'

Then why didn't he say hello to Annie Sugden? That was the thought that came into Amos's mind as he turned away to attend to other customers. The phone rang, and he went to answer it. 'I have a call from Rome,' said the operator. 'Is Miss Zorelli there?'

Amos was flustered. 'She . . . er . . . no . . . she's at the auction.'

'I beg your pardon?'

'She's not here,' Amos said, gathering his wits. 'Ask the caller if I can take a message.'

There was a pause and then after a few clickings and buzzings, a voice with an American accent came on. 'Hello? You say Miss Zorelli is out?'

'She's at the auction,' Amos ventured. 'Who is it speaking?'

'The auction is still in progress?'

'Oh aye. Three days, it'll last.' Amos decided to put out some bait. 'She hasn't bought what she's after yet.'

There was a pause, and a slight sound as if the caller had cleared his throat or suppressed a chuckle. 'I see. Well, will you ask her to call me when she has some news?'

'Whom shall I say?'

'She knows,' said the voice. Then, with open amusement, 'Tell her David Field called.' The line went dead.

Amos wrote it down. 'David Field . . . from Rome.' He went galloping into the kitchen waving the paper. 'She's had a call from Rome. David Field, that's who she's in cahoots with.'

'Who, what?' Henry said, looking up from a saucepan.

'The client in Rome that she's buying for – Miss Zorelli, I mean! He just rung up. David Field, he said. Ask her to ring me when she's got some news.'

'Amos!' Henry admonished. 'That's a message you took for Francesca. Ought you to be trumpeting it all round Grey Top's echo?'

'Oh!' Amos closed his mouth and put the paper down on the kitchen table. 'Well . . . I suppose that's true. All t'same, there is something going on and this Mr Field is the feller who sent her, you can bet.'

'Happen you're right. But the question of the moment is, are these potatoes done or shall I give them five more minutes?'

When he'd served the meal he had little appetite for it. He wasn't one to let himself be depressed over business matters, but on this occasion the blow was so unexpected that he couldn't help being downcast. He'd had such high hopes of averting the worst by means of the claim that Emmerdale had established rights to the land, but now all that would have to be put aside. He certainly wasn't looking forward to this afternoon.

When he'd helped Amos tidy up after the midday opening and had a bit of a wash and brush up, he drove up to Emmerdale.

Annie had the kettle on for afternoon tea, but on this occasion had set out no cake or scones. This was to be a purely business occasion. The rest of the household were already assembled, looking uneasy.

'This is the moment of truth, eh?' Joe said.

'Seems like it.'

'I can't get over it,' Sam said. 'Jacob never breathed a word of it to anyone! All those years, he were paying for the use of that field, and never let on.'

'He never was a man to talk about his affairs,' Annie said.

'But a bottle of whisky! Whatever could have put an idea like that into his head?'

'We'll soon find out,' Henry said.

A moment later they heard the sound of a car coming into the yard, and Joe went to open the door to Gerald Verney and his wife.

'Good afternoon,' Charlotte said, looking a little embarrassed. She'd insisted on coming because she wanted to keep the whole thing 'civilized'. She couldn't help feeling that Gerald wasn't handling this very well. It was true that they would soon be finished with the Hall and everything else to do with Beckindale, but there was no point in leaving in a bad atmosphere.

Annie offered chairs. The new arrivals sat down. Gerald had a briefcase with him which he now unzipped.

'I found, among my uncle's papers,' he began, 'this old letter, and clipped to it a pencil note which I presume he copied in ink and sent to Jacob Sugden, because you'll see a date and the words "sent 19/8/48" and his initials. These are photocopies, of course, but I can produce the originals if you insist. But I think in that case I should like the meeting to be in a solicitor's office.'

'Gerald,' Charlotte protested.

Henry accepted the two photocopies. Joe came and looked over his shoulder. One was a copy of a letter, well penned in a careful, round handwriting. The other was fainter – having been scribbled in pencil – but the date and initials stood out clearly. It looked as if old George Verney had roughed out his reply and then copied it in ink, at the same time initialling the rough.

'You'd better read it out,' Joe said to Henry.

'Aye,' Henry said, clearing his throat. 'This is from Jacob to Mr Verney, Annie.

> Dear Mr Verney, I am writing to inform you that I have taken up for use the land bordering the lane and up to the edge of Verney Wood. It has not been in use for some considerable time and seems a pity to let it go to waste. I hope you will not mind my taking it up in this way. The main stretch borders Emmerdale land so makes a good pasture for our herd. If you have any objections perhaps you will let me know. Yours faithfully, Jacob Sugden.

It's dated 18 August 1948.'

There had been silence while he read. Now Sam snorted. You could tell he was thinking what a nerve his son-in-law had had, to appropriate someone else's land in such a saucy way.

'Perhaps you'd read my uncle's reply, Mr Wilks?' Gerald suggested.

'Eh? Oh, yes, certainly. This one's dated 19 August.

> Dear Sugden, Pinch my land, would you? You've got a nerve. But you're right, I haven't the staff to farm it now the Land Girls have gone, so you may as well get the use of it. But I can't let you get away with it for nothing, so let's say a bottle of whisky once a year, the first one as soon as you can get to the off-licence and thereafter on rent day at the Hall – make a nice addition to my New Year celebrations. Yours etc., George Verney.'

'I never saw any such letter among Jacob's things,' Annie said.

'He probably didn't bother to keep it, Ma,' Joe said.

'If you doubt the authenticity – ' Gerald began.

'No, no,' she protested, 'that's not what I'm saying at all. Of course I accept that Jacob took on that field on the

94

strength of this arrangement about a bottle of whisky. It's just the kind of thing old Mr Verney would have done . . .'

'It's hardly a fair rent by today's standards, I think you'll agree.'

'Nay, it's nonsense,' Matt remarked.

'But it is a rent all the same. It established that the Sugdens are the tenants of the Verneys as far as that one field is concerned. You do accept that?'

'No choice, have we?' Henry said. 'We've never owned that land at all.'

'Is that the way the law would see it?' Joe asked despairingly.

'I'm afraid so, lad.'

'Well, all I can say, the law really is an ass! We've worked that land ever since I can remember . . . Looked after it, ploughed and sowed . . .'

'Joe, the truth is the truth,' Annie intervened.

'What are you proposing, then, Mr Verney?' Henry enquired.

'What are you offering?'

'You'll give us first refusal to buy?'

'I'm sure my husband would want you to have the field,' Charlotte Verney put in, to remind Gerald that he had promised to be reasonable to the Sugdens.

Gerald took his time before he went on. 'You do realize the price of land on the open market?'

'Not all that much,' Matt said, surprisingly. 'There's not a big demand for little isolated fields.'

'Oh, it's a little isolated field now, is it? I understood it to be a big, important part of your farm!'

'So it is,' Joe put in, with a little nod of approval at Matt. 'But it isn't that important to anyone else.'

'It would make a nice spot to build a house, though.'

Henry shrugged. 'Put it up for sale on that basis, if you can,' he said. 'But your chance of selling without planning permission is almost nil. And you won't get planning permission.'

'You can't be sure of that.'

'Reasonably sure,' Henry said in a calm voice.

'Come on,' Sam said, getting testy. 'How much are you asking?'

Gerald said: 'I've had a long talk with my solicitor and he tells me that the going rate for agricultural land is a thousand pounds an acre and rising.'

Charlotte Verney drew in a breath. They'd been all through this over lunch and she'd extracted a promise from him that he wouldn't ask for anything like that. 'After all,' she'd insisted, 'they've been thinking of that field as belonging to them for years. You can't ask them to pay the top price for it – it'd be too unfair.'

But Gerald was enjoying himself. 'Twenty acres at a thousand an acre – that's twenty thousand.'

Joe shook his head. He'd been to the bank and been told they had no chance of getting so much on overdraft. If they were to find twenty thousand, it would have to be from a private finance house at formidable interest – which would be a terrible burden on the farm's earnings.

'Gerald!' Charlotte said in a pleading tone.

'But on thinking it over,' Gerald said, 'I came to the conclusion that, taking everything into consideration, I could settle for half that sum. My lawyer said I ought not to settle for less.'

'Ten thousand?' Dolly said, speaking for the first time.

'That seems a fair price to me. What do you say, Wilks?'

Henry looked at Joe. Joe raised his shoulders and let them drop, meaning: It's a lot but it's better than twenty thousand.

'Can we think it over?' Henry said.

'Of course.'

Charlotte was pink with embarrassment over the whole thing. 'We don't want to be grasping,' she put in. 'But things are hard with us too, you see. The tax does have to be paid, on the inheritance. You may think there's an awful lot of money, but there's an awful lot of death duties and an awful lot of other commitments, too.'

'My wife feels bad about it,' Gerald said. 'But the fact of the matter is, you're getting off easy.'

'You mean, only paying ten thousand for what's ours already,' Sam said with the light of battle in his eye.

'It's not ours in law, Sam.'

'Law! What's law to do wi' it, Henry? This lad here has never set foot in that field. But Joe and Matt and me, we've worked in it. And now all of a sudden it belongs to him and

96

we've got to pay him for all the work we've put in to make it what it is now. For don't forget – when Jacob took it over, it had three years' growth of nettles all over it.'

'That's neither here nor there, Mr Pearson,' Gerald said.

'Well, well, we have to talk it over,' Annie said, anxious to put an end to the bitterness. 'Can I offer a cup of tea before you go?'

Gerald would have said no, but was overruled by Charlotte who wanted to make a social occasion of it. Dolly did her best to make conversation and after a moment, Henry rallied and played his part.

'How's the auction going?' he enquired.

'No idea so far,' Charlotte said. 'The auctioneer seems quite pleased though.'

'When do the paintings come up for sale?'

'I'm not sure. I think on the last day. Why? Are you thinking of buying one?'

Henry felt an impulse of idle curiosity. 'There's one called "Dillingham Crags" that I wouldn't mind hanging over the mantelpiece in the Woolpack,' he remarked, and watched with interest for a reaction.

'Dillingham Crags? Is that a local beauty spot?'

'Aye, about eight miles away. Your ancestor painted it, Mr Verney.'

'What, mad old Oswald? I can't imagine anyone wanting to buy anything he did.' Gerald was quite uninterested in the idea.

'My partner's convinced that's what Miss Zorelli wants to buy.'

'Good luck to her, then.' Gerald sipped his hot tea. 'I'd have thought there were plenty of good painters in Italy without importing Oswald Verney.'

'It appears she's here on behalf of someone in Rome – a man called David Field.'

'Oh?' said Charlotte. 'That does seem odd – someone sending a buyer from Rome to get something at the Verney auction.'

'Field, Field,' Gerald murmured, turning the name over in his mind. 'That strikes a chord . . . I believe my father knew someone called Field. David Field? I think I heard him speak of him.'

'Really?' Henry said. 'Close friend, was he?'

'I can't recall. But anyhow, that accounts for it, doesn't it? I expect Dad mentioned Beckindale to him.'

'He probably stayed at the Hall, Gerald. Didn't you say that your father gave the address to friends who visited England?'

'That's it, of course. This chap Field probably stayed at the Hall some time in the past, and wanted a painting by old Great-Uncle Oswald as a memento.'

Henry thought it was rather over-sentimental to want a painting so much that you'd send someone all the way from Rome to buy it. The air fare to England, to say nothing of living expenses here, must be considerable.

But somehow Henry didn't feel inclined to alert Gerald to that point. Here was a man who was insisting on his pound of flesh; Henry couldn't exactly blame him for that, but it didn't make him feel cordial towards him. If there was something going on about some item in the auction, let Gerald see to it himself.

The Verneys finished their tea and took a polite leave. When they had gone Henry said: 'I don't think we've got any choice, have we? We've got to buy that field.'

'Ten thousand pounds,' grunted Sam. 'Outrageous!'

'No, it's very reasonable. Mind you, I think he only came to that price because his wife's been on at him. But whatever the reason, he's asking something below the current price so we ought to snap it up.'

'Huh,' Joe said. 'At that price, you can't exactly "snap". We'll have to talk to the bank.'

'I thought you already had?' Matt said.

'Oh aye, but then I were expecting to ask for twenty thousand. They may be a bit more friendly when they hear I only want half.'

Henry shook his head. 'They won't let you have ten thousand. If it was to extend the farm, or build barns, it would be different. But just to incorporate a field that has always seemed part of the farm . . . Nay, they won't be forthcoming. I reckon if we get three thousand on loan, we'll be lucky.'

'So what happens then?'

'We'll have to raise the rest ourselves.' Henry hesitated. 'I can chip in, of course. Let me just take a look at how I stand. But I have to warn you that I can't find the balance to bring it up to ten, not without having to sell shares – and this isn't a good time to be doing that.'

Matt met Dolly's glance. She looked away. Neither spoke, but Dolly knew then that when they discussed it later she would agree to putting their nest egg towards the buying of Top Twenty. It was goodbye to her hopes of a home of her own.

Chapter Eight

The last day came for the Verney auction. Amos, who had been keeping an eagle eye on Francesca Zorelli, knew for a fact that she hadn't bought anything as yet.

So whatever she wanted, it must be in the last lots. And those included the paintings by Oswald Verney. Driven by an obsessive need to know, Amos confronted her as she was going out to her car after breakfast.

'Off to the sale, Miss Zorelli?'

'Yes, indeed.'

'What are you going to bid for? Go on, you can tell me! It's got to be something that's left.'

'Now, that is very logical.'

'Is it,' Amos asked, ignoring her irony, 'that landscape by Mr Oswald Verney?'

'Certainly,' she said, with gaiety and something like elation. 'A charming old painting. *Molto elegante, molto carino* – '

'Eh?'

'That means, Mr Brearley, that it is charming, sweet – '

'You came all the way from Rome to buy a painting that's charming and sweet?'

'But certainly.'

She got into her Fiat and drove off. Amos stood in the light summer rain and watched her go.

It was beyond him. A painting by Oswald Verney . . .

He thought it over as he did the washing up, and came to the conclusion in the end that he had solved the mystery. He was going to tell Henry his conclusions, but Henry avoided him, saying he had to get to Hotten to see the bank manager with Joe.

Amos was almost beside himself. He felt he was privy to a great secret but couldn't find anyone to tell it to. But then, like a gift from Heaven, Gerald and Charlotte Verney appeared.

They had come, feeling duty bound, to be on hand on the last day of the sale. But as yet only odd lots of kitchen equipment and the like were being sold, so they had come out for a walk since the rain had stopped.

Amos saw them on the green, and came scuttling out. 'Mr Verney!'

'Hello, Mr Brearley. Turned out nice, hasn't it?'

'Yes, very nice. Listen, Mr Verney, I've got something to tell you! That painting – '

'What painting?'

'The one Miss Zorelli's going to buy! It must be a masterpiece!'

'What?' Gerald gaped at him, then glanced at his wife. 'But, Mr Brearley, from what I can gather, she's been showing an interest in something painted by my Great-Uncle . . .'

'That's it! Don't you see? He's an undiscovered genius!'

'Who? *Oswald?*'

'It's got to be that,' Amos cried, almost clutching the front of Gerald's jacket in his enthusiasm. 'Don't you see it all? She's in the know! It happens all the time, doesn't it? Painters are suddenly discovered as being great, after nobody's paid any heed to them in their lifetime. That happened to him – that one with the ear. At least, without it – '

'You mean Van Gogh?'

'That's him! Nobody thought owt of him while he were alive, now did they?'

'That's quite true,' Gerald said, moving away from Amos a little. 'I never thought of that.'

'So you've got to put a spoke in her wheel. If she buys Oswald's paintings, she'll take them out of the country. I read about that in the paper – masterpieces being lost to the nation.'

'Oh, quite,' Gerald said. 'It would be unthinkable if Great-

Uncle Oswald's paintings were lost to the nation.'

'Right, then, I leave it to you,' Amos said, feeling he had done his duty. He hurried back indoors, eager to finish his chores and get to the sale to see what happened.

Gerald looked at Charlotte. 'Crackers,' he said.

'I'm afraid so,' Charlotte agreed. 'Come on, let's see if they've decided to start on the harvest at the Groves' farm.'

'They won't start yet,' Gerald said. 'The grain has to dry off first, hasn't it?'

'My word, you are knowledgeable!'

He laughed. 'I think my farming abilities are about on a par with the Groves'! The manager of the Miffield business tells me they're not going to make a living out of the farm this year.'

'Oh, what a shame!'

'Well, not necessarily. It makes it all the more likely they will fall in with the idea of selling the lease. If they can be persuaded, it makes it far easier to sell the land to a syndicate.'

'Have you got an offer, then?'

'Well, there's a bit of a hint. Rashley says someone is showing an interest. But the Groves are a problem – the farm would take a big bite out of the bit that the syndicate wants to take on.'

'Oh dear,' Charlotte sighed. 'It's all such a problem, isn't it?'

Amos got to the auction about ten-thirty. He was in a lather, fearing that the auctioneer would already have disposed of the paintings. But no, the linesmen were just removing a pair of engravings, which had been knocked down for a hundred and fifty. Even that sum shocked Amos. A hundred and fifty – for a pair of things that weren't even in colour?

The auctioneer watched the next painting being set on the easel. He called the catalogue number then went into his spiel. 'Delightful local view by a former owner of the Hall, Mr Oswald Verney – "Breckstowe Village". Come along now, ladies and gentlemen, this is a piece of nostalgia. May I begin at a hundred?'

Amos looked at Francesca Zorelli, who was sitting about midway down the rows of seats. But she made no move.

Ah, thought Amos, she's waiting to get it for fifty pounds.

But no such thing. The auctioneer eventually began at fifty, went up by tens to a hundred, urged the buyers on to a hundred and twenty by fives, and sold at one twenty-five. And Francesca Zorelli had not even put in a bid.

Baffled, Amos watched her like a hawk. Surely if she knew Oswald Verney was an undiscovered genius, she'd buy up all his paintings? But she did nothing, until at last 'Dillingham Crags' was put up.

The auctioneer, determinedly cheerful, began again. 'Now, ladies and gentlemen, this charming landscape – a fitting partner to the others just sold. Shall we begin again at fifty?'

'Fifty,' said Mr Roberts from Hotten Library.

'Sixty,' said Owen Potter, who ran the gallery in Connelton.

'Seventy,' offered a dealer from London, who thought he might flog it to some exiled Yorkshireman.

'Eighty,' said Miss Zorelli.

Amos's heart thumped. So she wanted the Dillingham Crags painting, and none of the rest? What could be the meaning of it?

He looked about wildly for Mr Verney to see if he was going to withdraw the painting from the sale. But Mr Verney was nowhere about.

The bidding had reached a hundred and ten by the time Amos gave his attention to it again. It was with the London dealer.

'A hundred and twenty?' asked Mr Glossop, the auctioneer.

Francesca nodded.

Glossop looked at the Londoner. The Londoner nodded. 'A hundred and thirty. Shall we go on to one forty?'

Francesca nodded.

'One fifty?'

The Londoner nodded.

A dealer from Leeds, struck by their interest, flicked a finger. 'One sixty?' Glossop asked him, and received a nod.

So it went on, until one ninety. Then the Leeds dealer dropped out. He wasn't *that* interested. It went back to a little conflict between Francesca and the man from London.

When it reached two hundred and ten, the Londoner backed out. It was with Francesca for two hundred and ten.

'Two hundred and twenty,' cried Amos. Then nearly died of shock at his own temerity.

'Thank you, sir. Two hundred and twenty. Can I go on to two thirty?' He paused. 'Two thirty?'

Amos nearly died the death, Francesca made no move. Was he going to be left with a painting he didn't want, costing two hundred and twenty pounds he couldn't afford?

Francesca turned her head and smiled at him. He thought he would faint. She seemed to find it terribly funny.

And then, thanks be to the powers above, she said, 'Two thirty.'

'Thank you. Two forty? Do I hear it? Two forty? Anyone?' He looked at Amos.

But Amos had had enough. The idea that he might actually be left as the purchaser of this unknown genius – who might continue to remain unknown – was terrifying. Amos shook his head.

'Are we finished?' Glossop said. 'Very well. Sold, to the lady.'

A clerk stepped up to Francesca and asked for her name and address and how she wished to pay. She said she could come to the makeshift office to write a cheque. With an amused glance at Amos she walked away.

Amos stared hard at the painting as it was lifted down from the easel to be replaced by the next item. It still looked to him just like a landscape painted by a man who knew a little about handling paint but was no great master. Grateful at his escape, Amos went back to open his pub for the midday customers.

Sam Pearson came into the saleroom soon afterwards, to see if anything interesting was going on. The remaining artwork from the walls of the Hall was going quite briskly. Sam was a bit surprised that anyone would pay fifty pounds for a watercolour of Verney Wood, but there was no accounting for tastes. Then, all at once, a voice spoke up in the bidding that made him cock his ears.

He turned his head. A tall, middle-aged man was leaning by the door, bidding for a small woodcut of wildflowers on the riverbank. Sam stared at him. He turned back to look at the auctioneer, listening to the voice speaking from behind him. At last the woodcut was knocked down. 'What name, sir?' the clerk asked, approaching the buyer.

'David Annersley. I'm at Long Beck Cottage at the moment. I'll pay in cash.'

David Annersley? Sam could hardly believe it. But it was true – he had almost recognized the man the moment his eyes fell on him.

Now his interest in the auction had evaporated. Sam made his way out, but Annersley was nowhere to be seen. He hesitated, then moved off down the lane to the village, half-expecting to see him there. But there was no sign of him.

Amos looked up as Sam came in. 'Hey-up, Sam, did you go to the auction?'

'Just come from there.'

'What are you going to have?'

'My usual – half of cider. Listen, Amos, have you seen a feller around – he's staying at Long Beck, from what I hear?'

'Oh, him? Aye, he's been in once or twice. David Annersley.' Amos got the cider and put it in front of Sam. 'He said he used to live in Beckindale.'

'You've talked to him, then?'

'Oh, aye, just a word, you know. It's my duty as landlord of the local hostelry, to be conversational. D'you remember him at all?'

Sam frowned, looked grim, and took a big swallow. 'I only ask,' Amos went on, recalling his curiosity of a few days ago, 'because Annie seemed right took aback when she saw him.'

'Annie saw him?' echoed Sam, going red.

'Aye, t'other day. She didn't mention it to you?'

'No,' Sam said shortly, 'she did not.' He slammed his glass down on the counter and marched out, leaving half of his cider unconsumed.

Amos was amazed. First Annie nearly falls over backward when she sees David Annersely, and now Sam Pearson gets into a tiff about him.

His head was in a whirl. So much seemed to be happening. First there was the mystery of Miss Zorelli arriving out of the blue in Beckindale, then there was her interest in the paintings at the Hall, then there was the problem with Mr Verney and the field on Emmerdale land, and now there was a drama coming up over this fellow at Long Beck Cottage. Amos hardly knew whether he was on his head or his heels.

There was the usual lull after he'd served the first few eager customers. He went into the kitchen to light the oven, in which a shepherd's pie was waiting to be heated up, then was dithering over whether to shell some peas when he heard someone outside the back door. He opened it, to find Francesca Zorelli backing in with the Verney painting in her arms.

'Oh,' Amos said. He hadn't expected her. She usually ate lunch in either Hotten or Connelton. 'There's enough shepherd's pie for two,' he remarked.

'Shepherd's pie?'

'It's a . . . er . . . traditional dish. Meat and mashed potatoes.'

'I see. Thank you, but I shall go soon, and lunch in Hotten on my way.'

'On your way where?'

'To London, *naturalmente*. Now I have obtained what I came for, I am eager to be home again.'

'You came for that painting?' Amos said, eyeing it.

'Indeed. And since you have been so interested, I thought you would like to know why. It is a Caravaggio.'

'A what?'

'It is a painting by a Renaissance master – a Caravaggio.'

'It's a Verney,' Amos said. 'It's even got his signature on the edge.'

'That is only on top, the Verney brushwork.' She stooped to look at it. '*Che affronto!* That old nobody, to dare to paint over the work of a master!'

'Miss Zorelli, I don't get you. Anybody can see that's a view of Dillingham Crags – '

'Underneath it is a lost painting by Michelangelo Caravaggio – "The Flight of the Martyrs from the Lions" – painted in 1601 for the Dolciatto family and sold by one of their descendants to an English traveller in 1830 or thereabouts.'

Amos raised his brows and watched her. She seemed to believe what she was saying. She was all alight with pleasure and pride. 'And now,' she said, 'I take my leave. I wish to be in London in time for the Rome flight this evening.'

'But you can't just – '

'I'm packed already, Mr Brearley. I made ready this morning before I set out for the auction. If you would be so good as to bring my suitcase down? I will put the painting in my car.'

Helpless in the face of her briskness, Amos went up to fetch her case. When he came down, he saw she had wrapped the painting in layers of soft linen and put it in the back seat of her car. He put the case in the boot. She held out her hand.

'Bye-bye, Mr Brearley. Give my best wishes to Mr Veelks, and to the foolish Mr Verney who did not know the treasure he had under his hand.'

'Goodbye, Miss Zorelli. I'm sure I wish you a pleasant journey home.'

In a moment she had gone. Noises from inside the Woolpack warned him that Old Walter was banging on the counter for service. He hurried back in.

Well, no one could say he hadn't tried. If what she told him was true, Mr Verney had lost something valuable. But Amos had *tried* to tell him.

But what a story it would make for the *Courier*!

Dolly and Matt went to the Hall to see the end of the auction. It was a melancholy occasion – the house seemed gaunt and tired, with nothing left except dust and cigarette ends on the floor. The auctioneer's men were moving the last items out to the forecourt to be collected by the buyers.

As to the sale of the house and land, that had been withdrawn. Offers for the land had been received prior to auction, so that negotiations were now under way. Matt and Dolly buttonholed Mr Glossop to ask if there was no chance now of making an offer for the gatehouse.

''Fraid not,' he said. 'It looks as if it will be kept together with the house and other outbuildings. Were you interested?'

'We-ell . . . What sort of price might it have made?' Matt asked.

'Difficult to say. It's quite an attractive proposition for anyone who could invest about ten thousand in modernizing it.'

'Ten thousand to modernize it?'

'Well, less if you didn't want the very latest fashion, I suppose. I'd have thought that if you bought the lodge for, say, eight or nine thousand, and spent the same again on making it liveable, you'd have a property you could eventually sell for close on forty thousand.'

'We . . . er . . . didn't have that in mind. We were thinking of living there.'

'You were, Mrs Skilbeck? That's too bad. I don't think it'll be offered separately after all.'

So that was that. In a way, it mitigated the disappointment. Dolly had already come to terms with the fact that Matt would offer his money towards paying for Top Twenty. It could never have paid for the gatehouse, after all – although it might have been the basis of raising a mortgage. But the fact remained that if they had been able to use his six thousand, they could have started looking elsewhere.

'I'm sorry, love,' he said. 'Are you very disappointed?'

'Of course not. It was just an idea, any road.'

Matt sighed. 'Well, I've got to get back for milking. You want to come back with me?'

'I'll take a walk,' she said. 'It's a nice day.'

Her husband eyed her with concern but she summoned a smile. 'Get along with you,' she urged, and stood by while he got into the Land-Rover and drove off.

She strolled down the lane deep in thought. So they weren't going to have a place of their own, not now and not for the foreseeable future, unless they could find something to rent – and that was almost as unlikely as finding a golden egg under one of Annie's geese. There were cottages to let in and around Beckindale, but they were holiday cottages. Their owners, quite understandably, wanted a very high rent during the summer months. You could get a place at a very reasonable sum during January, February and March, but come Easter and the beginning of the influx of visitors, the money rose steeply.

So it was no use thinking of places to rent. And they couldn't buy.

What was to be done then?

As she walked, she stood aside to let cars go by as the dealers from the auction headed for home. The road was quite busy. She struck up the slope on a footpath to get away from traffic, and came out at last on the hillside above the river outside the village.

On the riverbank below her, two people were walking, arms wound around each other's shoulders.

There was nothing unusual in seeing two lovers out for a stroll. What struck Dolly as a little bit odd was the time of day. Most of the men in the district were hard at work at present. Matt, for instance, was milking. So was Joe, probably. Anyone not looking after their cows would be out in the fields, for the harvest was in progress.

It was certainly unexpected to see a young man out with a girl at four o'clock of a fine summer day. Despite herself, Dolly watched, wondering who it could be. At last a turn in the path brought them into full view.

Well, she should have known. It was Nicky Grove. If there was a man in the dales who wouldn't be at work, it was Nicky. Presumably it wasn't his wife with him, for Winn Grove would be lending a hand in her barley field. With a little moue of dismay, Dolly saw that the girl was that nice lass staying at Long Beck Cottage; Dolly had met her in the village shop the other day.

All at once Dolly gave herself a shake. Here she was, mooning about on the hillside inwardly reproaching Nicky Grove for not pulling his weight. And what was she doing, herself? Was she acting like a responsible wife and member of the Emmerdale household? No she was not!

She turned and struck back along the path until she came to a stile, and was soon crossing the disputed Top Twenty field on her way home. As she came into the yard she could hear the men's voices in the milking parlour, the hum of the machinery, the occasional lowing of a cow. She went into the kitchen.

Annie was taking muffins out of the oven. The appetizing smell filled the room. Sam was fussing with the kettle. 'We're late with our tea,' he complained.

'Well, we've all been popping in at the last day of the auction,' Annie soothed. 'It's quite a historic occasion. You can be ten minutes late with your tea on a day like this, surely?'

'Humph,' Sam said. 'Can't say I'm impressed. If that Gerald Verney were going to go on the same way, happen we're well rid of him!'

Dolly went up to him and linked an arm through his. 'I'll

make the tea, Grandad,' she said, and gave his arm a hug.

'Will you, lass?' he said, turning with a grateful glance.

She couldn't have expressed the surge of happiness that went through her. It was best just to busy herself with little domestic chores. She made the tea and began to set the table while Annie fetched the cold meat and salad from the larder.

'Is that all we're having?' protested Sam. 'We had cold at dinner-time too.'

'In hot weather like this, Dad, I thought you wouldn't mind.'

'Busy doing summat else, I suppose?' he said, with an angry glance.

'I . . . yes, I have been busy,' Annie said, surprised. Her face was flushed from dealing with the oven, but from the way her father was eyeing her you'd think it was guilt on her cheeks.

He sat down in his usual chair and said nothing more until the men came in from the milking shed. They washed at the sink. 'You got home safe and sound, I see,' Matt teased Dolly, for she had been known to take a wrong footpath before now.

'Aye, Dolly doesn't cavort around when she should be at home,' Sam remarked.

'What's the matter, Grandad?' Joe asked as he sat down. 'Pigeons been eating your peas again?'

'It's nowt to do with my vegetable garden,' Sam said with cold dignity.

'Oh, so there is summat wrong?'

'That depends on how you look at things. Let them that has guilty conscience think on right and wrong.'

Joe looked at Matt, who shrugged. When Sam got into a state of indignation, it was usually over something Joe had done or left undone. But this time Joe could look into his heart and declare he was guitless. He was too busy at present to be 'up to' anything, as his grandfather termed it.

'I haven't a clue what you mean, Grandad,' he said.

'Happen you haven't,' Sam said. He turned his head to look at his daughter. 'But your mother knows!'

'Dad!' Annie exclaimed, in protest but with a look of dawning enlightenment.

'You mean it's Ma that's in your black books?' Joe asked, amazed.

'I say no more,' Sam said. He rose, pushing aside his plate. 'I don't want any tea.'

'Now, Dad, don't be silly – '

'Silly? Silly? Is that a word to use to me, when you think of your own behaviour over that man?'

With that, he stormed out, banging the door behind him.

Chapter Nine

Henry Wilks had been to Hotten on the last day of the Verney auction, to talk to the solicitor. With him he took the photocopies of the letters dealing with the letting of the Top Twenty field.

'Dear, dear,' Mr Jenkins said, taking off his glasses when he finished reading. 'What an extraordinary arrangement!'

'I'm told it's quite in keeping with the character of the old George Verney. What I want to know, Jenkins, is – is it legal?'

Mr Jenkins put on his hornrims again and glanced through the note from Mr Verney. 'Oh yes,' he said, 'quite legal. It constitutes a contract, however odd and informal. Jacob Sugden admits that Verney owns the land when he asks permission to farm it. Mr Verney grants permission but asks for rent. Jacob, apparently, paid the rent regularly.'

'It seems so. Old Mr Pearson says he took the whisky to the house on one or two occasions, and Joe Sugden says he remembers the like. As a rule, I think, the whisky was handed over with the rent on New Year's Day, when there was a sort of event at the Hall for all the tenants, though that was discontinued after young George Verney got married.'

'There you have it. Custom hallowed the arrangement. The rent was paid in kind. You say no further bottles were delivered after the younger Mr George Verney went abroad?'

'Well, I never heard anything of it and Joe says they just let the whole thing slide. You see, the family had taken it for granted it was just a sort of New Year present to Verney –

they didn't think it needed to be *paid*.'

'In that case it seems Emmerdale are in arrears for a couple of years' rent.' Mr Jenkins allowed himself a faint smile. 'But that apart, the situation is quite straightforward. Mr Verney – Gerald Verney, the heir – is the owner of the field. You must make some new arrangement with him about rent.'

'There's no question of that. He doesn't want rent. He wants to sell out. We talked about it and he said he'll take ten thousand.'

'Did he, indeed. That was very reasonable. Conscience troubling him, no doubt.'

'I think it was his wife, chiefly, who got him to name a price like that. On the face of it, that field was ours. She understood that. Everyone thought so. I think she felt a bit awkward. So Gerald suggested a price lower than the actual cost of agricultural land – although you'll appreciate, Mr Jenkins, that he's got scant chance of selling one isolated field at current asking price.'

'Quite so, quite so. He has to be reasonable. It's in his own interest. Do you need my advice, Mr Wilks?'

'We-ell, I'd like an opinion. Would we get the price down if we made threatening noises?'

'We've nothing to threaten about. His solicitor would soon put him wise. My opinion is to close with his offer rather than cause any ill-will by argument.'

Henry sighed. 'I thought you'd say that.'

'Would you like me to write to the Miffield Trustees?'

'May as well.' Henry took out his handkerchief to wipe his brow. 'I don't know what I'm getting in a lather about. It's just that we could do other things with ten thousand pounds if we had it to spare!'

'Can I be of any assistance in raising the money?'

'I think we'll manage. We don't want to overstretch our credit so we're trying to do it out of funds. With money costing what it does just at the moment, we don't want to borrow.'

'Very wise. Well, Mr Wilks, let me offer you a cup of tea. I know things look a bit dreary at the present time, but I've always found that a cup of Earl Grey and a ginger snap can do wonders.'

Henry had meant to get back in time to see the end of the

auction at the Hall. He felt it would be only civilized to do so – to shake hands with Verney and say goodbye on good terms. But in the event he was too late. The last few pieces of furniture were being loaded into a van, and the auctioneer, Mr Glossop, was getting into Mr Rashley's car as Henry drove up.

'Ah, Mr Wilks! Were you intending to bid for something? If so, you're too late.'

'Nay, I thought I might find Mr Verney here.'

'He has been here, but he's gone now. A bit depressing, I suppose, to see the place in this state.'

'Made much in the sale?'

'About what we expected,' Glossop said cautiously.

'Nothing suddenly appeared as a dark horse?' Henry asked, thinking of Francesca Zorelli and her interest in the sale.

'No, nothing. We got more or less what we expected for the Sèvres and the Hepplewhite, we did rather better with the bric-a-brac and rather worse with the Victoriana. Swings and roundabouts, swings and roundabouts.'

'How about the house and land, Mr Rashley?'

'We've got offers on the land.'

'Mind telling me if a syndicate is after it?'

'I haven't any objection. Yes, a small syndicate is looking at it as an investment, but there are problems. One of the tenants wants to buy his freehold, and then one of the farms is let at an absurdly low rent. It was let go, rather, so I didn't dig my toes in when I negotiated the rent. Now, alas, it's proving a difficulty.'

'That'll be the Groves at Holly Farm,' Henry surmised.

'Well, as to that, I'd rather not say.'

'Please yourself,' Henry said, 'but the Gimbels let the place run down and it's common gossip that the young woman who got the lease only had limited funds. Well, I'd be sorry to see a City syndicate take over, Rashley. No matter what mistakes a young farmer makes, at least he or she has a personal commitment to the land.'

'I rather wondered that Emmerdale didn't bid for Holly Farm,' Rashley murmured. 'Would have been handy for you –'

'Handy if we'd had the money! But we didn't want to rent

it, and we couldn't afford to buy it.' Henry stifled a sigh. 'Just as well, as things have turned out. We found another use for any spare cash lying around.'

Rashley gave him a nod of understanding. As Verney's agent, he knew of the altercation over Top Twenty. 'Well, goodbye for the present,' he said. 'I expect you'll see me in the village from time to time until the sale of the premises is complete.'

'Goodbye, Mr Rashley. 'Bye, Mr Glossop.'

His watch told Henry that Amos would already have opened for evening business. He was guiltily aware that he hadn't been around much today; Amos would be quite justified in reproaching him. Henry drove back into the village and put his car away.

'Mr Wilks,' Amos greeted him with suppressed excitement, 'I've solved the mystery!'

'What mystery?'

'About the painting, of course.'

Henry suppressed a groan. Not again! He'd had enough irritation for one day: having to agree to pay out money for Top Twenty, learning that a syndicate was after the Verney agricultural land . . . And now Amos was going to start again about Oswald Verney's landscapes.

'Have we got anything in the larder for the evening meal?' he enquired, thinking that if he were doomed also to one of Amos's economy dishes, he would have to drown his sorrows in whisky.

'There's enough cold ham for the two of us. But that's not what – '

'The two of us? Francesca not joining us?'

'She's gone, Mr Wilks!'

'Gone?' This was sufficiently unexpected to shake him out of his depression. 'Where?'

'Rome.'

'That were a bit sudden, weren't it?'

'You might say so,' Amos said. He took hold of the top button of Henry's jacket and drew him near . . . 'She took the painting with her!'

'What painting?'

'It's a Cab*bage*-o.'

'A what?'

'She said. A Cab*bage*-o. An old master.'

'There's no such thing. Cabbage-o? You've got the name wrong, whatever she were talking about.'

'Nay . . . well . . . happen it were a Carabbo. Just a minute, I wrote it down the minute she'd gone – for my piece for the *Courier*.' Amos drew Henry into the back room, where he picked up his notebook from the table. There, in the midst of some scribbles, was the name underlined several times. Amos picked up the notebook and frowned over it. 'Er . . . Caravano,' he suggested.

'There's no old master called that either,' Henry said. 'She were pulling your leg.'

'Mr Wilks, I'm not one to be taken advantage of,' Amos intoned. 'She told me she were leaving, and as I'd been so interested in what she wanted to buy, she'd give in and make a clean breast of it. She'd bought a . . . a . . .' He hesitated. 'I think that's a "j" . . .' Henry glanced at it. Amos's finger was pointing. 'A . . . d . . . j . . . o.'

'Amos! Could she have said . . . Caravaggio?'

'That's it,' cried Amos. He seized his pencil and began to write in capital letters.

'Nay, Amos, it's spelt with two "g's" – '

'Oh, them funny foreign names! All right, two "g's". That's what she said – Caravaggio.'

'At the Verney auction?'

'Aye.' Amos consulted his aide-memoir. 'A lost painting, of the Martyrs Fleeing from the Lions, by this Caravaggio.'

'Did you see it? What did it look like?'

'It looked like Oswald Verney's painting of Dillingham Crags.'

'You what!'

'She said as the masterpiece were underneath. But mind you, that's the bit that's peculiar. I mean, why would Oswald Verney use somebody else's old canvas to paint his own works? I mean, he were a rich man – he could afford to buy new canvas and all that.'

'But don't you see,' Henry said, sinking down on a chair, 'it all fits wi' what we were told about him. There he was, a rich old chap, fond of his own opinion and disapproving of the great painters. I can tell thee this, lad, I don't know much about Caravaggio but I'll take a bet his "Martyrs Fleeing

rom the Lions" had a lot o' naked men and women running
around. And Oswald were strict – a pillar of the church. So
he'd feel fully justified in painting over an "immoral" scene
like that.'

'But I still say he'd have bought new – '

'Don't you remember, Amos? We were told he got rid of
many great works of art. We all took it to mean he threw
them out or destroyed them. But happen he painted over
some of them.'

'Well, I were at the auction, Mr Wilks. And Miss Zorelli
showed no interest in any other Verney landscapes. It were
that one – "Dillingham Crags". She bid for that.'

'What did she pay?' Henry asked.

'Well, I thought she'd gone round the bend! She paid two
hundred and thirty.'

'Two hundred and thirty?' Henry felt a sudden surge of
glee. 'Two hundred and thirty pounds for a Caravaggio?'

'Aye, but then you see, I thought it were an Oswald
Verney, so I dropped out.'

'*You* bid for it, Amos?'

'I thought somebody ought to,' Amos said, looking
perplexed and scared. 'I nearly got landed wi' it!'

'So you dropped out. At two hundred and thirty pounds.'

Amos nodded. 'I expected Mr Verney to be there to
withdraw it from t'sale. I warned him, you see.'

'You did? You told him it was a Caravaggio?'

'Nay, Mr Wilks, I'd no idea o' that. But I told him Miss
Zorelli were interested in that painting o' Dillingham Crags
and suggested he should take precautions. Only he never
turned up.'

'And the painting went for two hundred and thirty
pounds.'

'You keep saying that, Mr Wilks. As if it intrigues you.'

'Oh, it does. It does. Because if that painting really is a
Caravaggio, it's worth about a thousand times that amount.'

'Oh, I guessed it were probably worth a lot.'

'I mean it literally, lad. I think a Caravaggio would be
worth two hundred *thousand* pounds at today's prices.'

'You're joking!'

'I'm not, you know. Not that I know the art world, but I
read about the auctions in *The Times* – and great works of art

115

go for fantastic prices. This one is a missing work: collectors and galleries all over the world would probably give their eye teeth for it. And you know what?' Henry said, with a sudden wide grin, 'Gerald Verney were sharp enough to screw ten thousand pounds out of us for a piece of land that we'd been tending for over a quarter of a century and regarded as our own. But right under his very nose, a sharper lass were taking away a piece of property worth, happen, a quarter of a million.'

'I just . . . can't come to terms wi' it . . .' Amos gasped. 'Money like that – '

'And I'll tell thee summat else, Amos. That quarter of a million wouldn't have been included in the sum to be taxed for death duties, because the painting's been discovered post-probate. He could have had it all – a quarter of a million!'

'Mr Wilks!' panted Amos.

'Aye! And you tried to tell him, didn't you, Amos?'

'I did. More than once. I said to him, I said, "That Miss Zorelli knows summat." But he wouldn't listen to me.'

'Let's have a whisky, Amos! We deserve summat, don' we?'

Amos followed him into the bar, looking dubious. 'I don' exactly see that, Mr Wilks. I mean, we haven't done anything, have we?'

'No, it wasn't up to us to do anything, really, was it? I wasn't our affair.'

'No-o, but . . . Shouldn't we do summat now?'

'Such as what?'

'Tell Mr Verney.'

'I've no idea where he is.'

'At the Feathers in Connelton, I s'pose.'

'All right, Amos, you ring him up.'

'Me?'

'Ring him up and tell him Miss Zorelli bought a painting she claims is a Caravaggio. He never listened to you before but he may listen to you this time.'

'Well, I – '

'There you are, lad.' Henry handed him a tot of whisky. 'Here's to you.' Amos looked bewildered, raised his glass, sipped, and set it down. 'You've got a grand story for the

Courier, haven't you? It's better even than our hold-up when Pip and Steve shut us up in the cellar. At least this time you keep your dignity.'

'Well, that's true, Mr Wilks.' Amos brightened. 'And as to ringing him up and telling him . . . I don't see there's much he could do, is there?'

'Not much.'

'He could get hold of Miss Zorelli, happen. But she said she were going straight to the airport.' Amos glanced at the bar clock. 'She's probably on the plane by now – she said she were taking the evening flight.'

'She may be at the airport. He could have her paged, I suppose. But if I were Miss Zorelli, I wouldn't answer any call to come to any telephone.'

'Could he . . . send the police?'

'Why should he? She hasn't done anything illegal.'

'It's a bit sharp, though? Buying a painting for two hundred and thirty when she knows it's worth a thousand times as much?'

'There's an old saying, Amos – *"caveat emptor"* – it means, let the buyer beware. In this case it applies to the seller too. If you put stuff up for auction – '

'You ought to take advice about what it's worth.'

It was only much later, in the middle of the night, that Henry Wilks sat up in bed and had a thought. A work of art of so much importance ought perhaps not to be allowed to leave the country. Sometimes when it was suggested a great painting was to be sold, the government refused an export licence.

If it had been known that Miss Zorelli was carrying a Caravaggio, she would no doubt have been stopped by the customs officers. But all the papers connected with the sale described the painting – correctly as far as most of the world knew – as a landscape by one Oswald Verney of Beckindale. She had paid two hundred and thirty pounds for the Oswald Verney. No one had had any reason to stop her.

Possibly, if Amos had rung Gerald and told him his tale, Gerald might have been able to alert the customs officers. But Amos had decided against ringing Gerald. Having been given the brush-off a couple of times, he'd no wish to court the same treatment again.

Henry lay down again, punched his pillow to make it more comfy, and composed himself to sleep. Happen he ought to feel sorry for Gerald Verney, but somehow he just couldn't.

Amos had intended to keep the story under wraps until it came out in the *Courier* with his byline. But somehow it slipped out, so that in the next few days it became a common talking point in Beckindale. In the evenings, when the men came in from the fields, they sat over their pints and took some black humour from the tale; there they were, working like beavers to get the grain in while the weather lasted and rather envying Gerald Verney. And Gerald Verney, though by no means a pauper, wasn't quite so much to be envied.

'Got egg all over his face,' was the general opinion.

The slow process of selling and buying the Top Twenty field went on. Dolly had by now resigned herself to the loss of Matt's inheritance. He found her one morning at church time, sitting on the side of their bed in the attic room.

'Dolly? You ready? We're just going.'

'Coming,' she said, but without getting up.

He came in from the doorway. 'You all right?'

'Perfectly. I'm just thinking.'

'What about?'

'About us having a place of our own.'

'Ah, love.' He came and sat beside her, putting an arm round her shoulders. 'That's off, for the time being.'

'No, I don't think so.' Her voice was firm and cheerful. She turned her head to look at him, and he saw determination on her bright face. She flicked what she was holding. It was a tape measure. 'Ever measured up this room?'

'Can't say I have. Why?'

'It's quite a good size. And a nice shape.'

'I suppose it is. I've never looked at it, really. It's just a bedroom.'

'Ah,' she said. 'Now that's the start of the whole of my thought process.'

'Eh?' said Matt.

'Your old bedroom is empty, isn't it?'

'Aye, of course.'

'It's a spare room – that was one of the romantic things you said to me when you proposed – that if we got wed, it would give Annie back her spare room.'

Matt laughed and hugged her. 'You can't deny it was true. So was the other thing I said – that you're a lovely lass.'

'Oh, I'm not just a pretty face,' she said, pushing him off so that she could wag a finger at him. 'What I was thinking was – why don't we move into your bedroom?'

'Why should we?' he countered. 'I thought you liked this room.'

'I do, Matt, I do! So much so that I'd like it as a sitting-room.'

'I'm lost,' Matt said.

'Look, love,' she said, springing up and making gestures to illustrate her points. 'If we move the bed into your old room, we could have a couple of chairs – a sofa, happen. And a TV of our own, and a radio. And happen even a little table with an electric kettle so we could have a cup of tea or coffee when we wanted it. What d'you think, love?'

Matt was nonplussed.

'Don't you think it's a good idea? I thought you'd jump at it.'

'Oh, I think it's grand. It's just that . . . We'd have to ask Ma.'

'Of course, Matt. But she'd agree.'

'And then she'd have to persuade Grandad.'

'How does he come into it?'

'Well, you know how he hates any kind of change. And just at the moment . . .'

She sighed. 'Aye, just at the moment he seems more than usually tetchy.'

'He'll get over it. He always does in the end,' Matt reassured her.

'I certainly hope so. I've never heard him so short with Annie.'

'I dunno what it's all about,' he said. 'Come on, love, let's get down or he'll be cross about being late for church.'

'But you will help me to talk to Annie about this idea, Matt?'

'Of course I will. But come on now. If we delay him any longer, Grandad's liable to burst into flames.'

After church, Henry caught up with Annie. 'Did you see Gerald Verney in church?'

'Yes, he told Mr Hinton he'd like to come to service as a sort of farewell to the village.'

'More likely he's come back to Beckindale to get away from reporters in London. They caught on to the story in the *Courier* on Friday – Amos had the nationals ringing him up by Friday lunchtime!'

'He's in his element, isn't he?' Annie said with a smile. 'He'll absolutely love it when we get this celebration going.'

'What celebration is that?'

'I want to discuss it with you, Henry. Do you know that it's twenty-five years next week since Amos took over the licence of the Woolpack?'

'Never!'

'It's true. Dad mentioned it. Dad's fond of Amos. I think most people are, in their way. He's become part of the village.'

'And that's no mean feat, in only twenty-five years,' Henry said with irony.

'Nay, Henry.' She laid a hand on his arm. 'You're never made to feel unwelcome, surely?'

'Not unwelcome, no. But unassimilated – yes, I'm sometimes reminded that though I have my uses, I'm not quite a native of these parts.'

'I'm sorry. I certainly always think of you as being a Beckindaler.'

'And that's the highest compliment you could give me, eh?' he grinned. 'Well, so what kind of celebration are you planning for Amos?'

'Nothing out of t'way. I thought we'd gather for a drink and make a presentation.'

'Of what?'

'That's where I need your advice. What would Amos like?'

'From you and me and Sam, or what?'

'We thought from the village in general.'

'Have you collected, then?'

'No, but I will – when I've a minute in the middle of the harvest.'

'Aye, it's a busy time. Happen you could get Sam to do some of the collecting for you.'

She hesitated and looked down.

'Summat wrong, Annie? He seems very stiff with you just at present?'

'It'll pass,' she said, 'like everything does . . .'

'Come and have a drink,' he suggested. 'Cheer you up!'

'I don't need cheering up,' she replied, with a smiling shake of the head. 'But I'll take you up on it all the same – though I've got to get back to serve us dinners by one.'

The drinks came, but Annie hardly seemed to notice. She was looking out through the open door to the tables and chairs set in the sunshine of the forecourt. Henry's glance followed hers. Taking a seat at one of the tables was the visitor staying at Long Beck, and with him was his daughter.

For a moment it seemed as if she was going to go out and speak to them. But at that moment Nicky Grove came up, pausing to chat with Pru. After a few words he came in. 'Two halves of ale and a pint, please, Amos,' he ordered.

'Coming. Henry, could you lend a hand?' Amos begged.

Henry excused himself to Annie and went to take up his post in the bar. 'Amos, does Annie know that feller from Long Beck?' he murmured as he pulled the ale for Nicky Grove.

'I imagine she does. They came face to face about a week ago and she seemed to recognize him like a shot.'

'Who is he?'

'Name of Annersley. Used to live on a cottage on the Verney estate.'

'I never heard her mention the name.'

Joe arrived, rather later than he'd intended because he'd had to stop and talk with the contractor who was hiring out the combine harvester. He looked vexed.

'Summat wrong about the combine?' Annie asked.

'No, that's all laid on for next week.'

'What's up, then?'

'It just gets my goat,' he burst out, 'to see Nicky laying on the charm like honey on bread.'

'Fancy the lass, do you, Joe?'

'Not if she's the kind to make a show of herself over a married man.' Joe swung round to take a look, then turned back. 'Oh, give me a pint and let me drown my sorrows. And pour a half of cider for Grandad. He'll be along in a moment.'

But the cider remained untouched. Sam Pearson arrived a few minutes later but, on seeing David Annersley sitting with Pru in front of the Woolpack entrance, he turned on his heels and walked away, his stiff back depicting outraged indignation.

Chapter Ten

Joe got the combine started on his barley at six the following Wednesday. It would be only a one day job – Emmerdale didn't have a big spread of arable land, only two or three fields under foodstuffs. But that was a busy day, so that he fell into bed exhausted.

On Thursday he had to go into Hotten to sign some intermediary document about buying Top Twenty. Although it wasn't a market day, habit took Joe's steps by the Market Hall, where you could often fall into chat with the manager and hear some inside information about forthcoming sales.

To his astonishment, he found Nicky Grove there. 'Shouldn't you be in your yard getting your grain into the silo?' he asked. 'The contractor told me he'd get it all moved by trailer today.'

Nicky made a sound of annoyance. 'Time enough for that this afternoon. I felt I had to get away for a bit.'

'Away?' Joe said. 'In August?' His tone said, 'One time when you ought to be on the farm is August.'

'Oh, you don't understand,' Nicky said, his handsome face crumpling in an expression both huffy and plaintive. 'Winn's always on at me!'

'She's every right, if you ask me,' Joe replied. 'This is no time for you to be strolling round Hotten.'

'That's what's wrong with farming. No time. You're either whacking yourself out with work or sleeping to get over it.'

'When was the last time you ever whacked yourself out?' Joe grunted. He walked on, annoyed at having wasted words on him.

'Where you going?' Nicky asked, falling into step.

'Cup of coffee, then I'm for home.'

'Aye, come to that, what are you doing in the big city when you should be at home putting your grain into the silo?'

'I were here on business with a lawyer. And if you're going to say I'm neglecting summat at home, I'll remind you I've got Matt to stand in for me, not a little slip of a girl on her own.'

'Go on, Joe, give us a lecture. From what I hear you weren't always a model of uprightness yourself.'

'Never said I was. But nobody can accuse me of ever having neglected the farm. Not even for a pretty girl – and I've known a few.'

'That's what's wrong wi' you, really, isn't it?' Nicky said in a conversational tone. 'Gets up your nose that Pru Annersley won't show an interest.'

'Is that why you're in Hotten at this time of day?' Joe asked. 'Expecting to see her?'

'An' if I am?'

'Nothing. I just thought you'd have a bit more sense. She's only in Beckindale on holiday. In a week or two she'll be gone, and it'll be all over.'

'I don't know so much,' Nicky murmured.

To Joe's annoyance, he followed him into the self-service coffee bar. Short of turning and walking out again, there was nothing Joe could do – and as he felt in need of coffee, he saw no reason to let Nicky Grove drive him out.

In a moment or two they were settled at a table with their cups. Nicky had a large squishy cream doughnut.

'She's loaded, you know,' Nicky remarked.

'Who? Winn?'

'Naw!' Nicky almost guffawed. 'All Winn's money is tied up in Holly Farm. Nay, I meant Pru Annersley – or at least her Dad.'

'What did you do, ask outright?'

'All right, be high-minded! 'S a matter of fact, he told me all about it hisself. He makes agricultural tools. Oh, aye, there's money there.'

'I'm not really interested, Nicky.'

'Have it your own way. Listen, farms allus need capital, don't they? Bit invested in Holly Farm wouldn't do any harm.'

'But didn't I hear . . . I'm sure you said yourself . . . a bloke

123

came from Miffield Estate and seemed to be pulling a long face?'

'Aw, that were just Winn's view. 'S far as I can make out, he came and looked around and said he'd be in touch. But I went to a solicitor and he said that if we've got a lease, there's nowt the Miffield Estate can do.'

'Did you show him the lease?'

'We-ell . . . no . . . The lease is in Winn's name.'

'You mean you went to a lawyer and talked about all this without discussing it with her?'

'Why not? If you look at things in the normal way, the man would be the leaseholder. Taking things at face value, that is – any lawyer's going to think the farm's in my name, isn't he?'

Joe shook his head. 'Can't you ever be straight about anything, Nicky?'

'Aw, come on, there's no need to be so high and mighty! What's going on between your Ma and Mr Annersley?'

'What?' Joe gasped.

'Summat's up. I were standing talking to him and Pru on Sunday outside t'Woolpack when your Grandad walked up and walked away again, wi' a look like daggers. And your Ma went quite pale – I saw her.' Nicky finished his cream bun and licked his fingers. 'And Annersley looked a bit queer, I tell thee – as if he wanted to leap up and rush to comfort her.'

'You've got a great imagination, Nicky.'

'Oh, aye, happen it's just my imagination.' He got up. 'Well so long. Can't hang around here. I'm meeting someone.'

'Nicky –'

'What?'

Joe shook his head. 'Nothing.' What was the use, he asked himself as he watched Nicky stroll out to the pavement. He'd been going to ask Nicky not to mess up the girl's life – for she seemed a nice lass, with a gentle expression and eyes that lit up when she talked to her father.

By one of those odd chances that can happen, it was Joe who met Pru. He was walking towards the car park when she came out of it, having been driven to town by her father.

'Hello there,' Joe said. She was a sight for sore eyes, in a rather plain cotton dress, bare legs and sandals that seemed

124

to be two or three thongs. Joe didn't know that the dress had been designed in Paris and the sandals came from Italy – all he knew was that she looked a treat.

'I thought you'd be busy over your harvest,' she said.

'Past that stage.' He couldn't prevent himself saying, 'You'd think Nicky would be busy too.'

'Oh, he's got a contractor on that. He told me so yesterday.'

'Aye, that's true, I suppose. But that still leaves it for his wife to get into the silo.'

Pru had been slinging her shoulder bag over her arm. At his words she jerked so that the bag slid from her arm to the ground. Joe picked it up.

'What did you just say?' she said in a strange voice.

'I dunno. We were talking about the barley.'

'You said . . . that it still had to go into the silo . . .'

'Yes. Nicky's got a two thirds return – ploughed too deep. I reckon they'll be hard put to it for feed this winter.'

'They? You mean . . . Nicky and . . . his wife?'

Joe frowned. 'Is something wrong?'

'No, nothing. Not a thing.'

Then it dawned on him. Nicky had never told this girl he was wed. She, a stranger in the neighbourhood, had no way of knowing unless someone told her. And since almost at once she'd shown herself to be attracted to Nicky, no one had wanted to discuss him with her. Like Joe, people had taken it for granted that she knew.

Joe squared his shoulders. 'Her name is Winn,' he said. 'Winifred. A nice lass, keen to make a go of the farm.'

'Yes, I know.'

'You do? That's all right then. See you around, Pru.'

'Yes, I expect so.'

She walked on. Joe went to the Land-Rover and got in. He paused for a moment before switching on. Life was really rotten sometimes. Why should Winn Grove be saddled with a tyke like Nicky? Why should a nice girl like Pru Annersley fall for him?

With a shrug he set out for home. Nothing he could do about it, any road.

Nicky was waiting for her by the market cross, as arranged. When she avoided kissing him in greeting, he took it to be embarrassment about kissing in public. He linked his arm through hers and led her through the public park on the north of the market square, to a spot on the banks of the river which was shady and romantic.

'You look nice,' he said, drawing her down on the turf at his side.

'Thank you.'

'I got to Hotten a bit early. It seemed a long wait till you came.'

'Dad wasn't feeling like hurrying this morning.'

'You worried about him?'

'No, he's doing quite well, I think.'

'You seem kind of quiet.'

'I don't think I'm ever very talkative.'

'With me, you are.'

She made no reply. Under her fingers in the turf she found a daisy. She plucked it and began to pick the petals.

'She loves me, she loves me not,' Nicky intoned. 'You'd better make it come out right for us, Pru.'

'The question is, what's right?' She was thoughtful, then said: 'When you're not working at the farm, Nicky, who looks after it?'

'Eh?'

'I mean, you can't just keep locking it up and going away. What happens about the milk collection, for instance? And having feed delivered, and all that?'

'Well . . . There is someone there, of course.'

'Yes?' She waited. She wanted him to volunteer the information. If she had to challenge him with her knowledge it was the end between them.

'The fact is . . . I've wanted to tell you this for a while, Pru . . .' He might as well. It would have to come out in due course. If, as he hoped, he persuaded Pru to think of him as a future husband, there would have to be a divorce. He'd always known he'd have to tell her but he knew he could handle it. 'The fact is, Pru, I'm a married man.'

'I see.' She didn't seem surprised. It struck him she might already have guessed.

'I want to be honest with you, Pru. I've been wanting to tell you for days. Only, I was afraid – '

'Of what?'

'That it would make a difference. You see, love, when we first met, I never dreamed I'd get to feel like this about you. We were just friends at first – kidding each other a bit, you know, seeing each other for a walk or a drink somewhere. But now –'

'What now, Nicky?'

'I don't want you to think badly of me, Pru. A man can get trapped into marriage. All Winn ever wanted was someone to do the rough work about the farm – her farm. It just happened that I was around. I was fond of her, she wanted the marriage . . . You know how it is.'

'I just never thought you . . . You didn't seem like a married man.'

'I don't think of myself as a married man!' He was quick to seize the point. 'I've always felt more like a hired hand. And since I met you –'

'What?'

His fertile imagination was at work. 'I went to see a lawyer, Pru. The divorce is in hand. Everything's quite straightforward between Winn and me. We both know we made a mistake. It'll be a friendly parting.'

Pru threw away the remains of the poor little daisy. 'How do you know you're not making a mistake with me?' she asked, her mouth trembling.

He took her chin in his hand and made her face him. He gazed into her eyes with a look he'd always found telling in such circumstances. 'Do you think I am?' he demanded.

Tears came to glisten on her lashes. 'How can I tell?' she whispered.

'Listen, love, I know it's been a shock to you to hear about Winn. I told you because I wanted to say something else, something more important. I love you, Pru. I never thought I was going to feel this way, but it's happened. And because I wanted to tell you how I felt, I had to tell you about Winn. What I've got to find out now is whether you feel enough for me to stick by me.'

'Oh, Nicky –'

'I want no secrets between us. Everything open and sincere. I'd think you can tell when a person's sincere or not – can't you, love?'

'I . . . yes, I suppose so.'

'So I've told you about Winn. Don't tell me you haven' had a boy-friend or two.'

'But I never married any of them!' she struck in with mor spirit than he'd expected.

'Nay,' he said, taken aback that she would hit back even s little. 'I know there's a difference between having had a fev romances and getting married. I've explained – Winn wante it. And you see, I'd never been in love and never expected t be. It wasn't until I met you . . .'

'Oh, Nicky,' she said, melting.

'I can't ask you to marry me yet. That wouldn't be right. love you, I'm sure of that. But we have to give it time to grow don't we? Until you're as sure as I am. I felt I had to clear th ground because you – ' He'd been about to say, because yo were beginning to ask questions, but caught the words back 'Because you're so precious to me that only complet honesty will do.'

'Yes,' she said, looking up at him with affection.

'I'm quite happy to wait a bit to find out whether you lov me.' He paused, half-hoping she'd leap in with, 'Oh, I do, do.' But as she said nothing, he went on: 'Happen it'd be bes if we didn't meet for a bit. You'll be going back to Leed soon.'

'Oh, no,' she cried, grasping his sleeve as he made as if t scramble to his feet. 'Don't go, Nicky.'

He relaxed at her side again. She went on in apology: ' know I seem silly, not going along with you and saying I fee the same as you about things, but . . . it's been a bit of shock. You do understand, don't you?'

'It's not silly. You need to be sure, don't you?' He put a arm about her but didn't attempt to kiss her. Instead he dre her head to his chest and stroked her soft hair. That, he' found, was an effective way of making a woman feel belove and protected. 'We'll both give it time,' he said, 'we'll b patient, see what happens.'

She nodded against his chest. He gazed up at the heaven and smiled. He had no doubt about what was going t happen.

Amos Brearley was also in Hotten that morning, summone to a conference by his editor. The piece about th

Caravaggio had raised him in the estimation of Mr Towers. Look at it how you liked, it was clear that Amos had cottoned to something being planned by the Italian lady, and had been proved right.

'I hear Mr Verney was in Beckindale over the weekend,' Mr Towers said. 'Any come-back about the painting?'

'Well, he weren't pleased, Mr Towers. No, not pleased.'

'I thought you might like to do a follow-up piece. The nationals have followed it up, sent their stringers in Rome to talk to this Zorelli lass. She's shown the painting to some bloke at a museum and it's been authenticated.'

'"Authenticated",' Amos said, writing it down in what he fondly thought of as shorthand. 'Did they find out how she knew it were there?'

'Aye, that name you mentioned in your piece – David Field – he turns out to be an old chap who deals in pictures. Has a gallery on the Via Veneto. Seems he knew Gerald Verney's father, the one that sang in the opera chorus.'

'Mmm,' Amos said. 'And stayed at the Hall some time.'

'Aye, but get this, Brearley: he stayed at the Hall eight year ago!'

'I . . . er . . . I don't follow . . .'

'That feller saw the picture then, guessed there was summat under the oils Oswald had put on, and took the trouble to do a bit of research in Italy. I suppose these master-works have a history. Any road, Field traced back to find out what that old bloke bought when he was in Rome on the Continental trip he took. You know, the one that went in the early eighteen-hundreds. And he was fairly satisfied that what was under the Oswald Verney was a Caravaggio. And then – get this, Brearley – he waited eight years for the owner to die!'

'Good gracious,' said Amos.

'I want you to mention that in your piece. How this dealer waited eight years to get the painting, never breathed a word to poor George Verney that he had a masterpiece hanging in the dining-room.'

'In a way, Mr Towers, that were just as well. Because it would have been included at its real value, not its face value, in the probate – and Gerald Verney would've had to pay tax on it.'

129

'Yeh, but after all, tax is sixty per cent. Even after tax, Verney would have inherited forty per cent of a quarter of a million. Which ain't hay, Brearley.'

'No, it certainly isn't,' Amos agreed.

'The funny thing is, Carlotta Lee, that half-gipsy that does our Stars column . . . She foretold Gerald Verney was going to come a cropper.'

'I knew her Granny,' Amos put in. 'Used to drive about the dales in a van.'

'I know, you told me before. Can't say I put much stock in it myself, but we get a lot of letters about her. Just for the hell of it, I got her to cast Verney's horoscope, and you should have seen what she said! Treasures unseen, don't take things at face value, prepare for a loss that won't leave you poorer, someone from over the water will take advantage of you. It's uncanny how right she's been.'

'Well, as to that, Mr Towers,' Amos ventured, 'after my dreadful experience with the gunman –'

'The what? Oh, when you were held up. Aye?'

'I happened on Madame Carlotta in the corridor here, and she drew my attention to the horoscope for my birth sign in that week's paper. And do you know what it said?'

'What?'

'Angry strangers will threaten you. You may be in danger. A cool nerve will see you through. You will lose financially but gain in reputation.' Amos beamed at the editor. 'There!'

'Aye, seems true enough,' agreed Mr Towers. 'Well, if you think you can, incorporate a bit about Carlotta in your piece on Verney. It's all good for circulation.'

Ever since the hold-up and the subsequent conversation with Carlotta, Amos had been more than a little interested in the stars. If he himself didn't have a piece in the *Courier*, the first thing he turned to on receiving it was the horoscope. He'd even taken to watching Patrick Moore on TV, to try to make out where the zodiac figures were – but the astronomer talked too fast and went on about the surface of Saturn and other such difficult subjects.

All the same, Amos had a growing interest in the stars. Often, before locking up at night, he'd go out and gaze up at the heavens. He'd even got to the point where he could quickly find the Great Bear and the Little Bear, and was sure he'd recognize Orion when he came wheeling into the sky in the autumn.

On his way to the bus stop, Amos paused to look in a shop window. It was an antique shop, whose proprietor had bought some of the bric-a-brac from the Hall. But chief among the items on show was a beautiful old telescope, once the property of old Miss Ethel Verney, sister of the now famous Oswald. Miss Ethel had been a game old girl, it appeared; she'd had many interests, among them astronomy.

The telescope was a lovely thing – gleaming brass and wood. Amos pictured himself out in the courtyard of the Woolpack in the quiet of the night, training the lens on Cassiopeia. He was sure he could find Cassiopeia if he had a telescope. Mr Wilks bought a daily paper which from time to time carried a star map showing what to look for during the coming month; if Amos owned the telescope he would sneak a look at the map and then go out and find the constellations, and be able to know what life was going to do to him in the near future.

But there was no price tag on the telescope, and that was bad. Anything without a price tag was sure to cost a fortune. Sighing, Amos boarded the Beckindale bus when it came.

Henry had already opened for the midday clients and Old Walter was already installed with his first pint. There was nobody else in the bar except Annie Sugden, who was standing by the counter with her head bent, in deep converse with Henry.

It seemed to Amos they started guiltily as he came in. They certainly broke off their conversation.

This wasn't the first time it had happened recently. Amos was most put out. There was something being kept from him, and he was going to get to the bottom of it!

'Busy?' he said in a scathing tone to Henry as he opened the bar flap and went behind the counter.

'The usual rush,' Henry said. 'I think I can cope.'

'Certainly business won't increase if you spend your time chatting, Mr Wilks, when you should be working!'

'Nay, now, Amos ... Annie and I were only talking about the concert of the Hotten Musical Society this evening. I wouldn't mind going with her, but it's your night off.'

'Oh, don't mind *me*, Mr Wilks! I'm accustomed to managing on my own. Twenty years or more in the licensed trade –'

Henry broke in hastily. A few minutes more and Amos would work out that he'd been twenty-five years at the Woolpack, and the surprise would be ruined.

'Then you don't mind if I go to Hotten? I'll come back as soon as the concert's finished. They're doing *Carmina Burana.*'

'Can't abide them Spanish things,' Amos said. 'Bullfights and all that.'

'Bullfights?' Henry said, his mouth falling open. 'Oh, it's not *Carmen*. It's a choral work.'

'Well, you go, then, Mr Wilks. Don't put yourself out to hurry back. I'll go out and look at the universe.'

'Beg pardon?'

'The stars in their courses, Mr Wilks. The lofty procession of the Milky Way.' Amos made a gesture indicating the vastness of space. 'It's as well to be quiet and alone at times like that.'

'Quite right, Amos,' Annie agreed, taking part in the conversation for the first time. 'I just thought it was worth mentioning that I had two tickets. Dad and I were going to go, but he's backed out.'

Amos was about to abandon his hurt feelings at that moment, for he badly wanted to know what the trouble was between Sam Pearson and his daughter. Sam was one of those who, in anger, became more and more silent and disapproving. Amos had tried everything he knew, but he couldn't fathom why the old man was so upset.

Last Sunday, for instance. Joe had bought a half of cider for him, and Sam had got quite near the door. But then, all of a sudden he'd turned his back and walked away, as if seeing Annie in the Woolpack had affronted him.

And yet Annie had been in the Woolpack many a time, with Sam. So it wasn't just the sight of his daughter in the bar on a Sunday that had put him out. It was something else. But what? What?

Annie said goodbye and went off to get the midday meal for her family. Her father came into the inn about ten minutes later, half inclined to say that after all he would go to the concert in Hotten this evening. But he'd missed Annie; she had walked back over the bridge and taken the footpath by the time Sam had reached the riverbank.

'Do you happen to know, Sam, when Gerald Verney were born?' Amos enquired.

'End of World War Two, I should think,' Sam said.

'No, I meant the month and the day. For his star sign, tha knows.'

'Star sign? Don't hold wi' yon. The Almighty rules our lives, not the stars.'

'But the stars are important, Sam,' Amos protested. 'That feller on the telly, he says they all exert a pull – '

'But that's the force of gravity, Amos,' Henry put in. 'Every star exerts a pull on every other one.'

'There you are then.'

'Nay, not psychic, Amos – actual. That's what keeps the moon from flying out into space – gravity. And the orbits of the astronauts are – '

'You can't tell me it doesn't influence 'em in other ways,' Amos said. 'There was one on 'em . . . threw up all his work with Nasser – '

'With who?'

'Nasser . . . The Space Agency.'

'Oh, NASA! I thought for a moment we'd moved on to Egypt.'

'And that's another thing,' Amos said. 'They were great astronomers, were the Egyptians. Them pyramids – '

'What about the pyramids? Were they space-launching pads?'

'You don't take it serious, Mr Wilks, but I read a book as how there are pictures of astronauts on tombs to do with them Anzacs.'

'Aztecs, I think you mean.'

'Aye, them . . .'

Sam had settled at a table with his glass and the daily paper, withdrawing into himself. He didn't notice David Annersley come in. David approached the counter and nodded at Henry who proceeded to draw a half of ale, the usual order he got from David.

David turned to lean back against the counter, 'Good morning, Mr Pearson,' he said.

Sam looked up. His bright, light-blue eyes darkened with ire. He said nothing.

'I hope Annie's well?' said David Annersley.

Sam leapt to his feet. 'She wants nowt to do with you!' he cried, his voice coming out half-stifled as if he had difficulty speaking. 'And if you're owt of a man you'll get out of Beckindale and out of her life!'

With that he stormed out, knocking over his glass and leaving a spreading pool of cider on the table.

Chapter Eleven

It was necessary for Annie and Henry to resume the conference they'd been having about Amos's anniversary. She rang him later, to suggest a meeting at the vicarage, because of course Mr Hinton was closely involved in the project.

'I had a thought,' Hinton said. 'I happen to have a mail order catalogue. Perhaps we could get an idea for a present in that.'

Henry was intrigued to know what use the vicar could have been making of a mail order catalogue. Hinton, catching his querying glance, shrugged. 'Someone told me they had good offers for hobby equipment. I thought I might see a good microscope, at a reduced price. I've got one, of course, but sometimes when I've got a butterfly mounted it's difficult to take it all to pieces to put another in the viewer.'

'You can never get a whole butterfly on the stand of a microscope?'

Hinton smiled. 'Of course not. I'm sorry. When I said mounted I meant some part of it, prepared as a slide. That's the trouble isn't it: a man with a hobby takes it for granted everyone else shares his knowledge.'

Henry was glancing through the catalogue. 'Might be summat here,' he murmured. 'I've got the glimmerings of an idea . . .'

They discussed the amount so far collected. The inhabitants of Beckindale had shown a gratifying sense of obligation towards Amos. Henry looked at the items in the mail catalogue. 'They don't quite measure up to the sort of money we've got,' he observed.

'Well, let's all think it over and see if we can come up with something by tomorrow.'

They broke up the meeting. Henry went out with Annie. Her car was parked further down Vicarage Lane, so he strolled with her towards it.

'Annie,' he said, 'I don't want you to think I'm getting like Amos, but things don't seem right between you and Sam.'

'It's nowt, Henry,' she said, with a brevity that was almost curt.

He hesitated. 'Does that mean nowt at all, or nowt to do with me?'

She nodded in appreciation of the subtle difference. 'It's nowt but a prejudice on Dad's part,' she rejoined. 'It all goes back into the past, one of those things that seem to die away and be unimportant . . . But now Dad's getting in a state about it again.'

'Aye . . . There was a bit of a scene in t'Woolpack at midday.'

'Oh.' It was a sound of understanding. 'He didn't come home for his dinner. I waited a bit then sent Joe out looking for him, though goodness knows our Joe's busy enough these days without that. Joe ran him to earth in the Malt Shovel.'

'The Malt Shovel? Never tell Amos that! It'll cut him to the quick.'

'Well, Dad told Joe he went there because he could get a bite to eat. When Joe said, "There's food waiting for you at home," Dad told him to look and he'd see he was eating food. So Joe just left him there.'

'If you'll forgive me saying so, Annie, it sounds as if he's in the sulks!'

'He takes things to heart,' Annie corrected gently. 'He'll get over it.'

Henry could see he wasn't going to be taken any further into her confidence. He was puzzled and a little hurt. He'd thought he was a close enough friend to merit her confidence. And besides, he couldn't help guessing that the problem had something to do with David Annersely.

Henry had more or less resigned himself to the fact that he

135

and Annie were never going to get married. He'd asked and been refused once already. But he didn't fancy the idea of some other man turning up and meaning a lot to her somehow.

They parted quietly. Henry said, 'If there's owt I can do . . .?'

'Thank you, Henry. But it's between Dad and me.'

Her father was back home when she got there. When she asked him if he'd like something to supplement his snack at the Malt Shovel, he shook his head. 'I'll wait for my tea,' he said. He went out to pick some beans for next day's dinner, then pottered round the garden. At tea he had little to say for himself. When Joe and Matt teased him for taking his custom to the rival pub, he merely shrugged.

'These days you can't choose your company in the Woolpack,' he said tersely.

Annie was going to Hotten for the concert. Dolly sided the dishes for her, and assured her she'd make any tea, coffee or cocoa needed by the old man during the evening.

The concert was excellent. By common consent Annie and Henry didn't return to the topic of Sam's short temper. He drove her home but declined her offer of a late cup of something.

'I'll get back,' he said. 'I can take over the bar for the last few minutes if Amos wants to go out and do some star-gazing.'

Sam was alone, sitting straightbacked in his wooden chair with the paper folded on his knees.

'Enjoy the concert?'

'Yes, the singing was very good. You'd have liked it.'

'I'm not in the mood for gadding about at the moment.'

'Are you ready for your cocoa?'

'Yes. I'll have a biscuit too.'

When she'd given it to him he stirred for a moment in silence and then said: 'I may as well tell you. He was in the Woolpack this noon. It was bound to happen some time or other.'

She nodded. 'You've seen him around, surely.'

'Aye, but he spoke to me today. Addressed me direct! The impudence of it!'

'Dad,' she soothed, 'don't take it that way. Why shouldn't

he speak to you?'

'I'd have thought he knew better, considering the way we parted!'

'But that was years and years ago, Dad.'

'That doesn't cancel it out.'

She said very seriously, sitting down opposite: 'Does it never occur to you to think on your Christian duty over this? To harbour resentment –'

'Don't thee take it upon thyself to lecture me on Christian duty! When I think of what might have happened . . .'

'Dad, you were young yourself, once. Being young is no crime.'

'It isn't an excuse neither!' he riposted, glaring at her.

'Isn't it? Young and innocent – they go together, don't they? But you always took it for granted I were guilty.'

'You were a married woman, Annie.'

'Aye,' she sighed, 'I was. And now I'm a widow. That's how life deals with you . . .'

'You think that now you're free, that makes it all right for him to come sneaking back.'

'Now, Dad!' she chided. 'I can't let you use a word like that about him.'

The sound of the Land-Rover made itself heard. 'That's Joe,' she said, and went to the kitchen window. She wasn't sorry to have the conversation interrupted, and when he told her he'd found their sheep straying all over the road on his way home to Demdyke, she was quick to put on a coat and help him round them up.

They got most of them, although as a matter of fact three had got into Holly Farm's fields. Winn found them next morning, and penned them up for the present. 'You can take 'em round to the Sugdens after breakfast,' she told Nicky.

'Oh, can I? Thanks very much. As it happens, I've plans of my own.'

'What d'you mean? I thought you were going to get the plough on the barley field this morning?'

'It'll wait. I've something else on my mind.'

'Listen, Nicky,' she said, her colour rising, 'that field's standing empty. Joe Sugden said to me the best thing to do is get it turned over as soon as possible and then get the grass seed in.'

'Oh, Joe Sugden, Joe Sugden! Who is he – God Almighty? The field can wait a day or two, can't it?'

'But why should it? I don't understand you, Nicky. You and I have got to make a living off this land, so why don't you – '

'Well, that's the point, really, isn't it?'

'What is?'

'Whether we want to make our living off this miserable stretch of nothingness.'

'But we agreed that – '

'*You* agreed. I didn't get much of a say, did I?'

Winn turned away from the dishes she was setting for breakfast. 'Listen, Nicky, it's late, we've let the morning get away from us already. Don't let's waste time on the same old arguments.'

'As it happens, this is a different argument,' Nicky flashed. 'It's about my share in this farm. Anybody can see we can't make a go of it, any more than we can of the marriage. So what I want to know is, when I talk to the lawyer about a divorce, what arrangement am I – '

Winn jerked away from him. Plates went flying from the table to crash on the floor. She paid no heed to them. 'Divorce?'

'You must have seen it coming. We can't go on like this. We've nowt in common.'

She made a great effort, took a hold of herself, then sought for words. 'So you want out, do you?'

'Yes, and I want what I put in.'

'Put in?'

'My share of the proceeds.'

'What do you mean, put in?' she cried. She kicked at the broken crockery. 'That's your share! You've put nothing in, not even hard work. You've no right to anything and you know it!'

He saw he had gone the wrong way about it and changed tactics. 'Come on, sit down,' he said. He took her wrist and drew her to a chair. 'We've reached the end of the line, Winn. No use rowing over it.'

'All right,' she said, jerking free. 'The end of the line where marriage is concerned. But you've no claim on the farm.'

'Property held in common – '

'We don't hold it in common. I bought the lease with my money.'

'It don't work like that, love,' he told her. 'By law I'm entitled to half the matrimonial property.' As she opened her mouth to protest he swept on: 'No use griping about it – that's what women's lib has brought you! What's yours is mine and what's mine is yours – and as I've nowt, the courts'll grant me half of what's yours. Half the farm. Unless you like to buy me out.'

She stared at him, wordless.

'I hate to make things awkward,' he said, 'but I need the money.'

'If I scrape any money together to give you, it means I've nothing to run the farm with.'

'Well, six of one, isn't it? You won't be able to run it when I'm gone. You can't manage alone.'

'I can get a man in.'

'Paying him with what? Come on, love, be sensible. We're splitting up and you won't be able to make a go of it. Let me have some cash and be shot of me.'

'Why d'you want the cash so urgently?' she asked, frowning at him. 'What are you up to?'

'I'm up to getting out of this daft situation: married to somebody who keeps me drudging – '

'No, it's more than that.' She was shrewd enough to read him now she'd been shocked into doing so. 'It's a woman, isn't it?'

'There's no woman. I've just got itchy feet. Time to be moving on, as the song says.'

'Nay, there was something in the way Joe Sugden looked a time or two ago – '

'Oh, him! A lot he knows!'

'So there is something to know?'

'I never said that.'

'But all of a sudden you want a divorce? I was all right as a meal ticket, but suddenly you've got someone better in tow – is that it?'

He hadn't meant her to be so quick on the uptake. Although she knew he had an eye for the girls, she had in the past tried not to acknowledge it.

'Let's get this out in the open,' she said. 'You want a

divorce to marry someone else?'

The last thing he wanted was for Winn to find out about Pru. If, in her honest, blundering way, she should go to talk to Pru about things, it could be awkward. Winn in the flesh was not at all the demanding selfish wife he'd depicted her. Pru was waiting for him now, at the road junction. He wanted to be able to go to her and suggest they go away together. But to do that he had to have some ready cash.

He was unaware of a shadow touching the edge of the open door of the kitchen, a shadow that drew away again to avoid detection.

'There's no one else,' Nicky said. 'On my honour, Winn.'

'Your honour?' She actually laughed with something like genuine amusement. 'You suddenly spring the idea of a divorce on me this morning then in the same breath ask for your share of the communal property when you know you've scarcely done a stroke of work here since we came. And you think I'll take your word of honour?'

'Listen, Winn, you and I haven't hit it off. I'll admit I haven't had any enthusiasm for the farm but I went along with it because I was fond of you. It's not my fault my feelings have changed. I've a right to go away and make a new start. But I swear to you I'm going on my own – there isn't anyone else. I wouldn't do a thing like that, take your money and go after another woman.'

'You swear it?'

'I swear, Winn.'

There was a gasp of horror, and Pru Annersley stepped into the doorway. 'Nicky!' she cried. 'How could you?'

'Pru!'

'You . . . you . . .' She turned and fled.

For a moment Nicky was aghast at what had happened, unable to move.

'So much for your word of honour, Nicky,' Winn said, tears of anger and disgust welling in her eyes.

He turned and ran after Pru.

'I wouldn't bother,' Winn called, 'she heard enough.'

Pru raced for home like a deer. She heard Nicky behind her at first, calling to her to stop, but she paid no heed. She almost fell into the garden of Long Beck Cottage, where her father was settled in a deck chair with *The Times*. He started up as she came stumbling in.

'My dear *girl*! What's wrong?'

'Nothing – he – I –'

'Did someone frighten you – molest – ?'

'No! Oh, Daddy!' She flung herself on his chest and burst into tears. 'He's horrible! Horrible! And I thought he was so good and gentle!'

'Who? What's going on?' Then, with growing realization, 'The young man? Nicky?'

'He's . . . I didn't tell you . . . he's married, Daddy.'

'Oh, lord – !'

'And I just . . . just heard him. He told me . . . she . . . he said she . . .'

'Didn't understand him?' David suggested, stroking her hair.

'Don't laugh at me!'

'I'm not, my dear. It hurts too much to be laughable. Poor lass, poor lass. Come on, now, come indoors and wash your face. Come along.' He led her in, took her upstairs, pushed her into the bathroom. Then he went down to make tea. It was a long time before she reappeared, and in that time David Annersley did some thinking.

So much emotion, so much misunderstanding. And where did it arise? From a lack of plain dealing. He himself was to blame here. He had been too wrapped up in his own affairs to pay any heed to what was happening to his teenage daughter.

He had faltered too long without making any step towards Annie. He had wanted her to make the first move, to throw open her arms in welcome. Then he had allowed Sam Pearson's furious disapproval to deter him. But that was over now. He had come here to see Annie again, and he would do so. But first he had to comfort and reassure Pru. Poor child, this was her first serious love affair – and what a disaster it had turned out to be.

But she was young, she would recover. David knew this was true from his own experience. For he had a broken love affair in his own past.

When Pru came down she was pale and drawn, but composed. She took the tea he poured, sat down at the kitchen table, then looked at him as she sipped. 'I've been an awful fool, haven't I?'

141

'I don't know.'

'I overheard him talking to Winn – that's his wife. He didn't turn up where we'd arranged to meet so I walked up to the farm. I thought I might as well meet her, you see.'

'And what did you hear?'

'I can't tell you. It just showed him . . .' she gulped . . . 'quite different. All at once I . . . Well, it's over.'

'Good.'

'Good?'

'When something is over, that's the time for a new beginning.'

'Yes.' Tears glinted for a moment but she blinked them back. 'I suppose I'll look back before long and find it all very funny.'

'Perhaps not,' he said, taking her hand. 'It's never very funny when you're hurt.'

They fell silent. He glanced out of the window. There, at the gate of the garden, he saw a figure he knew. 'Excuse me, Pru,' he said, getting up, 'I've got to have a talk with someone.'

It was as if Annie had tuned in to his thoughts of earlier on. There she was at the gate, soft brown hair gleaming in the sunshine, skin lightly tanned by the summer weather, the colour of her eyes reflected by the thin cardigan thrown over her shoulders.

'Hello, Annie,' he said.

'Hello, David.' She smiled. 'It's a bit silly for us to keep on trying to ignore each other, isn't it?'

He opened the gate and came through into the lane beside her. 'I never tried to ignore you. I was waiting for you to make some sign you wanted to know me.'

'I've been remiss. I should have made an old friend welcome.'

'Hard for you,' he said, linking her arm through his and strolling away with her. 'Your father seems to be strongly against it.'

'I don't understand his attitude. I can only apologize for it.'

'But it does make things awkward, Annie. He more or less warned me off yesterday.'

'Is that what happened? He was in a right state later on.'

She stopped and turned to face David. 'Listen, I want you and your daughter to come to tea this evening.'

'Oh – Annie – do you think that's wise?'

'He can't make a fuss when we've a guest in the house. We must make a start, mustn't we? Will you come?'

'Aye, lass,' he said gently, 'I'll come.'

They talked for a while, then he offered to drive her back to the farm, as it was time for her to get mid-morning coffee for the men. When the big Citroën showed up in the yard, Sam's face went thunderous. He was digging in his garden, but dropped the fork to glare at her as she walked towards the house.

'You've been to see him?' he exclaimed.

'If you mean David Annersley – aye, I have. You must know that's his car.'

'I'm surprised at you!' he said. 'Have you no thought for Jacob?'

She sighed. 'I never did owt against Jacob, Dad. And I've done nowt to be ashamed of. Then, nor now.'

So saying, she walked past him to the house.

Henry turned up for coffee, bringing with him the assurance he had solved the problem of Amos's anniversary present.

'What is it, then?' Matt enquired. 'Typewriter?'

'Nay, something more interesting than that. I want it to be a surprise. Wait till you see it.'

'You're sure he'll like it?'

'Well, if he doesn't,' Henry said, 'I'll buy it off him. I quite fancy it myself!'

Dolly offered cake around, then said, 'Should I get the rhubarb tarts?'

'Nay, those are for tea. We're having guests for tea.' Annie looked round the kitchen. 'I've invited David Annersley and his daughter.'

There was a tense silence. Henry looked at Sam. Sam's face went scarlet, but he said nothing.

To break the awkwardness, Joe said, 'I gather he used to live on Verney's estate.'

'And how do you gather that?' Sam enquired.

'I had a chat with him a few minutes ago – met him standing by that foreign car of his, looking at the Groves'

143

farm. Did you know Groves are likely to pack it in?'

'Really?' Henry said. 'I did hear rumours Miffield Estate were trying to buy them out – their lease, I mean.'

'Mr Annersley seems interested in the Hall. Half inclined to buy it, I thought.'

Sam snorted, but said nothing.

'Did you use to know him, Grandad? His father worked for Verney.'

'I know nowt about the man,' his grandfather said, almost in a snarl.

The atmosphere was volcanic. Everyone looked at the old man with apprehension, except Annie who said: 'Yes you do, Dad.'

He glared at her.

'It's no use sitting there letting old quarrels eat away at you. It's a long time ago and nowt's to be gained by dwelling on them.'

'You've dwelt on his memory, though. That's plain enough.'

'Now, Dad – '

'And he on yours. Why else is he here?' Sam's voice rose. 'Seems to me the only one who isn't remembered is Jacob, your husband. I never thought a lass of mine would turn against her husband when he was cold in the grave!'

'Grandad,' Joe put in, with trepidation, 'don't let's cry up Dad too much. I've heard you say more than once he had a lot of faults.'

'But a wife should be loyal! She should know where her duty lies!' Sam pointed at his daughter. 'But no sooner is that man back in the village than you're running off seeing him!'

'You know that's not true. He's been here a long while and today's the first – '

'So you say!' He rose to his feet. 'Happen that's why he's interested in buying Verney's – to come back showing off to a place where he was ordered out by those who saw through him!'

He stamped out. The rest of the household sat in stunned silence. Henry, more embarrassed than he would ever have thought possible, hastily swallowed the remains of his coffee and took his leave. Matt and Joe escaped out to their work on Clissold's barley fields. Dolly was left with Annie.

144

'I'll clear up,' she offered, and busied herself with the crocks. Annie sat in listless inactivity, so unlike herself as to be positively eerie. By and by Dolly took a chair beside her. 'Don't upset yourself,' she murmured. 'He didn't mean it.'

'Oh, he did. That's what makes it so sad.'

'But he'll come round.'

'I thought so. But if he can still speak like that after so many years . . .' Annie shook her head. 'It's all in the past!'

Dolly understood only too well how the past can come back to haunt us. 'Your father seems to think it was important.'

'From his view, I suppose it was. I look back now and I realize that happen he thought . . . I weren't long married, Dolly, and Jacob had his problems wi' the farm. One day he up and left.'

'Left?'

'Oh, it was all a misunderstanding. He came back by and by, puzzled that we'd taken it so hard. But while he were away, it put me in a difficulty. Dad worked for Verney's then, and there weren't anyone to help. So David Annersley stepped in. Without him, I might have gone under.'

'Stepped in to help with the work?'

'Oh yes – I don't mean it in any other way! But I must be honest and say I found him – well, he were a sunnier temperament than my Jacob. He made everything seem different.' She sighed deeply. 'I might be nothing but a middle-aged widow now, but in them days I had my share of romantic notions and happen if David had waited and stood where I couldn't forget him, I'd have wanted to run off wi' him.'

Dolly was about to say, 'You, Annie? Never!' But this was a different Annie they were talking about – younger, more vulnerable. 'So what happened?' she prompted.

'Nothing. David was my friend and I was his. Then he went away. But, you see, there just must have been more to it than that because I kept his letter.'

'He wrote to you?'

'Before he left. I've got that letter upstairs in my trinket box. In a way, Dad's right. David meant something to me – otherwise why have I still got it?'

'But we all keep things.'

145

'Aye, and there's nowt in that letter to be ashamed on. He spoke as he felt and I don't think any person that saw his words would think the less of him.'

'Perhaps if you could express yourself like that to Grandad . . .?'

'I've tried.'

'I know, but – '

'I ought to try again, is that it?' Annie shrugged, nodded, and pulled herself to her feet. 'It's the best thing to do, I reckon.'

She went out. She knew where to find her father: in his workshed. It was his refuge in times of great trouble.

He turned as she came in, looking offended. 'Can't a man have some peace and quiet?'

'Not after an outburst like that, Dad. The others couldn't think what had come to you.'

'No? I'd have thought it were plain enough. I was reproaching my daughter with taking up again with a man who wanted her to break her marriage vows.'

'Oh, how can you!' she burst out. 'You know very well he packed up and left.'

'And why? Tell me that?'

'Because . . . because he could see it were no use – '

'Huh!' Sam snorted in triumph. 'Is that what he told you?'

'He's never discussed it with me. What do you mean, Dad?'

'I ordered him off, that's what! I sent him packing! He'd not even the spunk to fight for you, lass, and I promised him a whipping if he tried to come between you and your duty ever again.'

'Dad!'

'I promised him a whipping if he showed his face again. And let me tell thee, Annie, I keep my promises! I keep my promises to the dead as well as the living – and though Jacob's gone I'll fulfil my obligation to him.'

'That's just wild talk – '

'I mean it. And why you should be so concerned for a man who ran away like a whipped cur, I'll never know.' He picked up the piece of wood he had been planing. 'And now if you don't mind, I've work to do.'

'Dad, don't close yourself up in this fairytale about – '

'It's not a fairytale. Ask him. Ask him if he didn't pack up and run when I told him I'd take a stick to him!'

He turned his back on her and began to push the plane along the wood. She could see he wouldn't say another word.

When she went into the kitchen Dolly had gone out. She picked up the phone and dialled the number for Long Beck Cottage. 'Can I speak to you, David?'

'Of course, what is it?'

'Not over the phone. Can we meet?'

'Say where and when?'

'I've got to get the meal. Can we say two o'clock by the beck?'

'In our old place? I'll be there.'

The sense of strain throughout the midday meal was hard to bear. She hurried out as soon as she could, and walked to the ruins of the old mill where she had so often spent quiet hours in her youth. David was there already, his long body propped against a tree trunk.

'Something's wrong,' he said. 'I can tell.'

'Well, something's not right,' she said ruefully. 'Dad is still behaving like a mule.'

'Perhaps you'd like to cancel your invitation to tea.'

'I don't want to let the past warp the future. We were friends, David. I want to be friends again.'

'If the truth were told,' he said with a sigh, 'we were more than friends. But I knew you would never leave Jacob, so I left. It seemed the best way.'

'Was that the only reason?' she ventured.

He pulled himself away from the supporting treetrunk to stare down at her. 'It's important, is it?' He thought a moment. 'I left because I knew I couldn't win. At the time I thought I was doing what old Mr Verney would have called "the honourable thing", but if I'm honest I have to admit it was because I was making no headway. You had the perfect defence.'

'Defence?'

'Your innocence, Annie.'

As she gazed at him with surprise in her face, he laughed. 'I mean that in the nicest way. You didn't even know I was trying to win you away from Jacob. He'd gone whizzing off on some prank of his own, and God knows you had good reason to be resentful and out to get some revenge on him. But no . . . It didn't even seem to occur to you.'

She gave a little smile. 'I think it occurred to me,' she said. 'I suppose if I were being as honest as you, I'd say I just didn't have the courage. I couldn't embark on an "affair". I can't be doing with deceit. I just . . . couldn't face it.'

'But that's what I loved about you, Annie,' he said. He reached out and took both her hands. 'And in a way, that's why I left you. I couldn't take on the responsibility of breaking up that . . . innocence.'

They stood for a moment face to face, hand in hand. Then she said: 'My father is saying you left because he chased you off.'

'What?' It was a little burst of laughter.

'It isn't true, of course.'

He was still chuckling. 'Not that Samuel Pearson isn't alarming in his wrath! But no – I'd already written to you saying goodbye. I don't suppose you remember that letter, Annie.'

'Oh, but I do,' she said in a soft tone.

'Well then, if you can remember? I put it through your door on Easter Sunday while you were at church.'

'Aye, I remember.'

'I was going that very day, but the trains were changed because of the Bank Holiday. I missed it at Hotten. So I stayed one more day, and on Easter Monday your father came stalking up to me outside the gates of the Verney Estate and told me to pack up and go. Or else!'

'I see,' she said. 'Now I see. You'd already decided to go. It had nothing to do wi' him.'

'That's right.' He smiled down at her. 'Does it matter so much?'

She coloured. 'I ought to be ashamed to admit it,' she said, 'but I wouldn't have liked it if you'd turned tail and run.'

Back home again, she went up to the bedroom and took the letter from the trinket box. She took it with her into the shed. Her father was hanging up his tools and generally tidying up for the day. He frowned when he turned to find her in the doorway.

'Didn't I tell you I don't want you in here?'

'I've come to show you something, Dad. You reckon you

saved my marriage by warning David off?'

'You're not denying it? I saw him outside Verney's gates and next day he were gone. You can't get away from that.'

'Do you remember what day it was?'

'What day? No, why should I?'

'You remember a lot about it. Don't you recall how it came about you were at Verney's?'

'Of course. I'd gone to see to the horses –'

'Aye,' she said. 'Hunt, weren't it?'

'Aye.' He stopped, looking at her. 'Easter Monday?'

'That's it. Now look at this.' She handed him the folded letter.

'I'll read nowt he wrote to you!'

'You will, Dad,' she insisted. 'You're a fair man. You need to see that what you do and think is fair. And I tell you that if you read that you'll see David Annersley had already decided to go when you spoke to him.' As her father made a movement of rejection she went on: 'It begins by saying that by the time I read the letter, he'll be on the train to Leeds. I've just spoken to him. He tells me the train timetable was changed that day because it was Easter Sunday. So he stayed one more day. Read it. Above all, look at the date. It's headed "Easter Sunday".'

She laid the letter on his workbench and went out. After a long moment of indecision Sam picked it up and unfolded it.

When, three hours later, Pru and David arrived for tea, Sam was polite to them. He said very little, because he was too upset and embarrassed to have many words. But the rest of the household were relieved. They'd been expecting some kind of outburst.

Annie made no attempt to see more of David after that gathering. They met by chance from time to time in the next few days, but she had much to occupy her. Harvest was almost over, it was time to start preparations for the Harvest Supper.

The task of gathering in the crops was coming to an end and Joe and Matt had been busy helping neighbours but, in the way of farmers, they had kept an eye on what was going on elsewhere.

'You'd have thought Nicky Grove would have got up on

that biggest field of theirs wi' the plough,' Matt observed.

'Oh, he's a lazy beggar.'

'But you'd have thought Winn would have got behind him, eh?'

This was true. Joe wondered if something had gone wrong with their tractor. If so, perhaps he could help. He wasn't bad with machinery.

He made his way to Holly Farm, to find the place strangely quiet. The milk herd were out on the higher pasture, quite a way off, but even so, there seemed to be nothing going on.

'Hello?' he called, walking across the yard and looking in at the back door.

Winn was moving about the kitchen. It had a strange air. 'Hello, Joe,' she said, 'come in.'

He saw that there were several packages on the kitchen table, wrapped in newspaper. They looked like ornaments or photographs. It suddenly dawned on him: Winn Grove was packing to leave!

'What's to do, Winn?' he asked, sitting on a wooden chair.

'As you can see – ' she gestured around, 'I'm going.'

'Bit sudden, isn't it?'

'I suppose so. But things happened suddenly.'

'Who's taking the farm, then?'

'Miffield Estate are putting in a caretaker manager for the time being. He's around somewhere, looking at the fields.'

'Where's Nicky? Haven't seen him around.'

'Oh, he took off. We had a row a couple of days ago. He took the van and scarpered – leaving me with no transport, but that didn't matter to him. He's done something like it before but he comes back, swearing he'll reform. This time he'll find no one to make his vows to – I'll be gone.'

'Winn!' Joe exclaimed. 'You mean he doesn't know about all this?' He jerked his head at the packages.

'Not a thing.' She smiled thinly. 'He was trying to winkle cash out of me when we quarrelled – said it was time we went our separate ways. And then this girl looked in and he took off after her and didn't come back.'

'Girl? He's gone off with a girl?' Joe frowned. 'But I thought he were interested in – ' He broke off.

'Pru Annersley, is it? No, she ran off and he went after to

150

try to sort things out – but I reckon he saw he'd cooked his goose there. So he went away to let things cool off, imagining I'd forgive him again. But not this time, Joe. This time I've had it.'

Joe looked concerned. 'Anything I can do?'

'Nay, Miffield Estate will sort everything. They were after me for the lease but I didn't want to sell. And then . . .' She sighed, and rolled a brass candlestick in a sheet of newspaper. 'When I realized what he'd been up to this time – trying to get money out of me so he could go with Pru Annersley – I just got to the end of my tether. I went into Hotten on the bus and saw the agent, told him he could have the lease, and the stock and equipment at valuation.'

'Where'll you go? What'll you do?'

'Dunno. I shall have a bob or two – I've not lost by the sale. Miffield wanted the place empty, y'see.' Her round face creased with weary resignation. 'Place is worth more empty of me than with me in it! There's an epitaph, eh?'

'Epitaph?' Joe said, alarmed.

'Only a manner of speaking, Joe. I'm not thinking of doing owt daft. He's not worth it.' Suddenly she gave a grim laugh. 'I'd love to be here when he gets back and finds Mr Warner in charge.'

'What happens to him then? I mean, when he left, this was his home, in a manner of speaking.'

'His things are still upstairs. Mr Warner says he'll give him a week or so to get himself together. But then it's *out*. They've done their homework. They've no opinion of him. They won't even hire him on if he asks.'

'He won't ask,' Joe said, shaking his head with muted amusement. 'He never liked the life.'

'No. Happen it was my fault for trying to get him to take to it. When I met him, Joe, he seemed . . . Well, it's no use saying I was misled. I'm not a fool I shouldn't take things at face value.'

'When are you going?'

'I've a taxi ordered for this afternoon. I'll be gone by six.'

'Oh, I could've taken you – '

'Nay, this is a busy time. It's kind of you to take an interest.' She turned to the dresser and picked up a bulky newspaper-wrapped item. 'This is a casserole of your Ma's –

she brought it over in t'winter when I had that two-day flu. Would you give it back to her and thank her for all her help? And thank you too, Joe, and Matt, for lending a hand so often.'

'It were the least we could do.' He took the package. He held out a hand. 'Well, so long, then, Winn. Shall we see thee again in these parts?'

'Shouldn't think so. I'll try for a dairymaid job, further north, happen. But don't tell Nicky if he asks. He's left me and I've left him and . . .' She gave a half-smile, half-sigh – 'Never the twain shall meet.'

'It's your decision, Winn. I'll say nowt if that's what you want. But won't he get a forwarding address from Miffield Estate?'

'I've asked them not to. You see,' and she looked sad at having to say it, 'he'd only want to get in touch to ask for half the communal property when the divorce gets going. Well, let him work for it. If he can find me, he can have it, if that's the law. But he's got to find me first.'

'Don't be bitter, Winn.'

'I'm not bitter. I'm just fed up of it. But I'll get over it, Joe.'

He left her, still busy with her packing. Perhaps it had been inevitable that those two should part. It was just a miracle that Pru Annersley had escaped relatively unscathed.

About a week later Nicky Grove was to be seen glooming about Beckindale, asking questions and getting no answers. He spoke to Joe once. Joe replied politely that he had noticed new people at Holly Farm but beyond that, he had no information.

'You're all in it with her!' Nicky growled.

'In what?'

'I'll have the law on her, you'll see!'

But the last that was seen of him was at a garage in Hotten, where he flogged the van for a smallish sum. Some said he'd taken a train. Others said he'd hitched a lift. But he was gone, and the general consensus was: Good riddance to bad rubbish.

Chapter Twelve

It was Amos Brearley's twenty-fifth anniversary and the time had come for the presentation.

Almost the entire population of Beckindale had come to the Woolpack on the appointed evening. Amos was beside himself. 'I never saw such a mob,' he flapped at Henry. 'Is there summat going on somewhere – a pop concert in somebody's field?'

'Not that I've heard of,' Henry said. He was perspiring. It was hard work dealing with all Amos's friends. He had promised drinks on the house after the presentation, and had no doubt he'd asked for all he was getting!

Henry had suggested nine o'clock as the hour for the event. He had asked the *Courier* to send a reporter. When this gentleman arrived, Amos nearly had apoplexy. 'He's my rival,' he hissed to Henry. 'What's he here for? To spy out my territory? He's got a nerve!'

Matt was watching Amos's reaction with amusement. 'Eeh,' he said to Dolly, 'he's giving Henry some stick!'

'He'll change his tune in a minute,' Dolly said. 'I bet nobody's ever thought of a thing like this for him before.'

'He's never been twenty-five years at the Woolpack before.'

'Oh, you! One more word out of you and I'll insist on bright green paint for our sitting-room.'

'Sitting-room. Can't get used to calling it that. It's always going to be the attic room to me.'

'I don't mind what you call it, Matt. It's a place of our own.'

'Aye, true enough. Not as good as a house, but we'll save up what we had to give away, and get a house some day.'

'Never mind,' she whispered. 'So long as we're happy, it doesn't matter where we are.'

Joe brought their drinks. 'I hope the speech is going to be soon. Amos is going berserk.'

'Henry's just taking a look around,' Dolly said. 'Here we go.'

Henry banged loudly on the bar. Amos glared at him. 'Mr Wilks! Isn't there enough racket in here tonight without that?'

'Don't fret, Amos.'

'I do fret! I'm running a business here.'

'And that's what this is all about.'

'What what's all about? Be so good, Mr Wilks, as to stop playing the fool.'

'Be quiet, Amos.'

'I will not be quiet!'

'Altogether, folks – tell him to be quiet.'

The entire crowd chorused: 'Be quiet, Amos!'

Amos's mouth fell open. He stared around him as if he were having a nightmare.

'I'm about to say summat, Amos, so please hear me out. This is the twenty-fifth anniversary of your taking the licence of the Woolpack, a momentous event we all felt couldn't go without a celebration. So . . .' Henry produced a long narrow package decked out in red foil paper and tied with silver ribbon. 'We beg your acceptance of this elegant object, formerly the property of Miss Ethel Verney of the Hall. With the best wishes of your friends.'

He held out the package to Amos. Amos drew away as if it were a serpent. 'Oh!' he gasped. 'Oh, heck!'

'Take it, Amos. It won't bite you.'

'What is it?'

'It's a telescope, as you'll find when you open it. Knowing your interest in the stars, we felt it would be a fitting gift.'

'A . . . a telescope. Like Henry Moore?'

'Henry Moore? Henry Moore's a sculptor – oh, you mean Patrick Moore. Aye, Amos, just like Patrick Moore.'

Amos began to pluck at the wrapping with fingers made clumsy by emotion. He took the telescope out of its case. Its sparkling finery of brass and mahogany dazzled him. At least, it must be the dazzle that was causing tears to brim over the rims of his eyes.

'Well,' he said. 'Well, I never . . .'

'Altogether,' cried Joe. 'For he's a jolly good fellow . . .'

The crowd broke into song. Amos stood clutching the telescope to his bosom, tears unashamedly streaming down his cheeks. 'Oh,' he was stammering, 'oh, f-fancy m-me getting a presentation!'

Alas, all good things must come to an end. Amos's euphoria vanished when he discovered the drinks were on the house. 'I suppose it's fitting,' he said, rather unwillingly, 'but it does seem a lot of folk to give away drinks to!'

'Go on with thee,' Henry cried. 'I'll pay, Amos.'

'You will?'

'Aye, let's live a little.'

As might have been expected, it was very difficult to get rid of the crowd at the end of the jollification. At last they filtered away, some of them still singing snatches of 'For he's a jolly good fellow.'

'Went well, I think,' Sam remarked as he was driven home by his grandson. 'I only hope it don't make him too big for his boots for the next few weeks.'

'You're joking,' Joe said. 'When he sees his name in the *Courier* as a recipient of a silver-anniversary gift, his hat size will go up several times, let alone his boots.'

'You were enjoying yourself, I saw,' Sam said. 'Sitting with David Annersley's lass.'

'Aye. She's a nice girl, Grandad.'

'No doubt.'

'Aw, come on. Admit you were wrong. He's a decent feller.'

'I quite agree.'

'You do?'

'I've just said so, haven't I?'

It was an improvement on his previous attitude, but not by much. However, Joe didn't pursue the matter. He simply said: 'Pru tells me they'll be going soon.' To which his grandfather made no response.

When David told Annie they were going, she was sad. 'I heard you were thinking of buying the Hall?'

'Oh, that was one of those passing fancies. It's too big.'

'I suppose so.'

'And besides . . .'

'What?'

'Your father is never going to like me, Annie. Not really.'

'Oh, that's nonsense – '

'It's true. After spending twenty-five years or more thinking ill of me, the best he can do is tolerate me.'

'But why should that matter so much?'

'I don't know. But it does, doesn't it?'

She took a moment before replying, but then had to nod assent. 'Isn't it absurd?'

'It's just the way things have gone for us. If we had been swept away by an irresistible tide of passion, it wouldn't have mattered, about Jacob or about your father. But you see . . .'

'We never got swept away?'

'I'm afraid not. At least, you never were. I was a bit hard put to it not to get carried off, but you were never in any danger. So I think it's best to call it a day, love.'

They were in the church, where Annie had gone to do the flowers for the following Sunday. They were speaking quietly, as befits a church. The air was cool, full of the earthy scent of black-eyed-Susans and African daisies.

David gestured to the surroundings – the rough walls with their plaques and memorials, the dark oak pews, the half-made flower arrangement on its brass stand.

'All that's important to you is here in Beckindale, Annie,' he said. 'I know it's no use asking you to go away with me, and I can't stay here because I don't fit in any more. So it's goodbye, my dear.'

He held out his hand. She took it. Even in that moment of sadness the practical part of her mind was noting that her fingers were stained with green juice from the flower stems.

'Goodbye, David. I'm glad you came back, even for a little while.'

He broke their handclasp, turned, and walked down the nave to the door. There was a momentary beam of sunlight as he went out, then it was gone.

For a long moment she stood in silence. Then, shaking herself, she picked up a yellow flower and began to trim it for the vase. The flowers had been supplied by Sam from his carefully-tended garden. As she put them into the arrangement she thought of him with fondness. Stubborn, brusque and forthright – but honest as the day was long. He hadn't quite apologized for thinking badly of her, but these flowers were his way of saying sorry.

She smiled to herself as she worked. In family life, there were bound to be misunderstandings from time to time. What mattered was that in the end family ties held firm, that honest speaking cleared the air. When she thought back over the last few weeks – the underhand dealing about the painting, the dishonesty of Nicky Grove – she was thankful that at Emmerdale life was simple. The values they held dear were the old ones of probity and good faith. And though some people might look superior if they heard those terms, she was prepared to defend them.

At Emmerdale, the life they led could be taken at face value – because they had no use for deceit, because they had no need of it. And so long as she was mistress of the household, things would stay that way.

Contemporary Romances

Once a Lover   **Diana Anthony**
Set in New York and San Francisco, *Once a Lover* is the moving love story of Lainie Brown, a young artist, and Jean-Paul Vallier, a blinded sports superstar. Then he regains his sight and Lainie fears she will lose his love. But she learns painfully and joyously why she is so worthy of Jean-Paul's enduring devotion.

Celebration   **Rosie Thomas**
Bel Farrer, a wine columnist, was a high-flying career girl. But beneath her glittering professional appearance was a vulnerable heart. Both the titled aristocrat bound by an ancient code of honour, and the reckless, carefree playboy claimed her heart and she had to make a choice.

Perfect Dreams   **Carolyn Fireside**
The world of high fashion, Hollywood and the jet set is the backdrop for this rich love story. Gabrielle Blake, a photographer's model, is independent, intelligent and lovable. Among the rich and famous men who fall in and out of Gaby's life is Terry Baron, a young journalist who finally rescues her when her career collapses. But is it too late for them to rescue their love for each other?

Perhaps I'll Dream of Darkness   **Mary Sheldon**
In this compelling and beautifully written story of love and obsession the lives of a teenage girl and a burned-out rock star entwine fleetingly – with disastrous results. Probing deeply into her characters' lives, Mary Sheldon creates a portrait of frustrated passion that leads to tragedy, and captures both the grace and terror of obsessive, idealistic love.

FONTANA PAPERBACKS

Winston Graham

'One of the best half-dozen novelists in this country.' *Books and Bookmen*.

'Winston Graham excels in making his characters come vividly alive.' *Daily Mirror*.

'A born novelist.' *Sunday Times*.

The Poldark Saga, his famous story of
eighteenth-century Cornwall

ROSS POLDARK
DEMELZA
JEREMY POLDARK
WARLEGGAN
THE BLACK MOON
THE FOUR SWANS
THE ANGRY TIDE
THE STRANGER FROM THE SEA
THE MILLER'S DANCE
THE LOVING CUP

His immensely popular suspense novels include

THE WALKING STICK
MARNIE
THE SLEEPING PARTNER

Historical novel

THE FORGOTTEN STORY

FONTANA PAPERBACKS

Fontana Paperbacks: Fiction

Fontana is a leading paperback publisher of both non-fiction, popular and academic, and fiction. Below are some recent fiction titles.

- ☐ SEEDS OF YESTERDAY Virginia Andrews £2.50
- ☐ SONG OF RHANNA Christine Marion Fraser £2.50
- ☐ JEDDER'S LAND Maureen O'Donoghue £1.95
- ☐ THE WARLORD Malcolm Bosse £2.95
- ☐ TREASON'S HARBOUR Patrick O'Brian £2.50
- ☐ FUTURES Freda Bright £1.95
- ☐ THE DEMON LOVER Victoria Holt £2.50
- ☐ FIREPRINT Geoffrey Jenkins £2.50
- ☐ DEATH AND THE DANCING FOOTMAN Ngaio Marsh £1.75
- ☐ THE 'CAINE' MUTINY Herman Wouk £2.50
- ☐ LIVERPOOL DAISY Helen Forrester £1.95
- ☐ OUT OF A DREAM Diana Anthony £1.75
- ☐ SHARPE'S ENEMY Bernard Cornwell £1.95

You can buy Fontana paperbacks at your local bookshop or newsagent. Or you can order them from Fontana Paperbacks, Cash Sales Department, Box 29, Douglas, Isle of Man. Please send a cheque, postal or money order (not currency) worth the purchase price plus 15p per book for postage (maximum postage required is £3).

NAME (Block letters) _____

ADDRESS _____

_____

_____